THE MARTIANS

Other Titles from Space Cowboy Books

Books

Mexicans on the Moon – Pedro Iniguez

Another Time: Time Travel Stories – Various Authors

Complete Poems 1965–2020 – Michael Butterworth

Simultaneous Times Vol. 3 – Various Authors

Simultaneous Times Vol. 2.5 – Various Authors

Simultaneous Times Vol. 2 – Various Authors

Simultaneous Times Vol. 1 – Various Authors

Garbage In, Gospel Out – Jean-Paul L. Garnier

Betelgeuse Dimming – Jean-Paul L. Garnier

Future Anthropology – Jean-Paul L. Garnier

Chapbooks

Micropoetry for Microplanets – Brian U. Garrison

Shelf Life – F. J. Bergmann

Mars Maundering – Denise Dumars

The Telepathy Machine – Jean-Paul L. Garnier

Time's Arrow – Jean-Paul L. Garnier

Utopian Problems – Jean-Paul L. Garnier

www.spacecowboybooks.com

THE MARTIANS

Transcribed from the Beyond

A Novel

EMILIE PROCHÁZKOVÁ

**TRANSLATED FROM THE CZECH
AND INTRODUCED BY
CARLETON BULKIN**

ISBN 979-8-9896308-3-7

Edited by Jean-Paul L. Garnier
Translated by Carleton Bulkin
Book design by F. J. Bergmann
Cover image: original cover of *Marťané* (*The Martians*, 1922)
by Václav Rytíř (1889–1943)

First English Edition | 2024

Space Cowboy Books
61871 29 Palms Hwy.
Joshua Tree, CA 92252
www.spacecowboybooks.com

CONTENTS

The cover image is based on the original artwork by painter and graphic artist Václav Rytíř (1889–1943) for the 1922 chapbook edition of *The Martians*. He studied at the Academy of Fine Arts in Prague and was influenced by Art Nouveau and Art Deco. Between 1916 and 1927, he illustrated a variety of books and magazines, as well as creating promotional materials and posters; a specialty was ex libris bookplates. Rytíř worked in the U.S. for a time under the name V. Knight, In 1935, he was elected vice president of The Bookplate Association International in Los Angeles.

INTRODUCTION

In the cataclysm of the First World War, Central Europeans had seen first-hand the fall of empires and technology's abuse by the powers of old. Drawing from the tradition of the utopian novel, fantastic literature took up these themes by reimagining science and society—more often, now, far removed from Earth in space and time—eventually acquiring the label "science fiction" from the late 1920s onward.[1]

Only a few years before the publication of Emilie Procházková's unsung pulp novella *Mart'ané* (The Martians, 1922), the regional map had been redrawn. Several new states emerged, among them the author's own Czechoslovakia, a previously unimagined amalgam of territory. The Habsburg Empire, in which Czechs had jostled with Germans for often limited cultural and political aims, had now been swept away.

---

1. As used here, "science fiction" describes a modern genre in which science and technology play a distinctive role in depicting an imaginary world, often extraterrestrial, that is meant to be plausible. English-speaking science fiction historians often begin the story from Hugo Gernsback's founding of the "scientifiction" magazine *Amazing Stories* in New York City in 1926. However, this disregards the often-fascinating backstory of literary responses to technological innovation—not only in English but more widely.

The term "science fiction" was coined in the U.S. in 1929 but has since been applied retroactively (William B. Fischer, *The Empire Strikes Out: Kurd Lasswitz, Hans Dominik, and the Development of German Science Fiction*, 5–6, 9, 15). For a survey of interwar American science fiction from this perspective, see Frederic Krome (ed.), *Fighting the Future War: An Anthology of Science Fiction War Stories*, 1914–1945. For one of continental science fiction, see Salvatore Proietti, "Science Fiction in Continental Europe before the Second World War." The modern genre emerged from a romantic speculative tradition that encompassed fantasy, gothic, utopian, and supernatural narratives.

So was the old class-based voting system; a new constitution established universal suffrage—and included women for the first time. Competing for these votes in the new republic were newly empowered mass parties. Agrarians and social democrats, but also industrialists, came to prominence. The emperor was no more.

Not only society but also science was advancing rapidly. Electricity, the telephone, and motor cars came into wider use. Telephones and electric doorbells began ringing in Bohemia prior to 1883, and the number of Prague telephone subscribers grew quickly from 187 in that year to 602 by 1888.[2] The city's first electric tramway set off in 1891. Only ten years later, the Präsident horseless carriage became the first factory-produced motorcar in the Czech lands (it was steered by handlebars).[3] Guglielmo Marconi (1874–1937) patented his wireless telegraphy device in 1896, and the same year saw the first mass-produced shellac records for gramophones. The Čihák brothers' monoplane, the first Czech-built airplane, was assembled in 1913.[4] In 1919, the British R-34 (based on a captured German Zeppelin) was the first airship to make a round trip across the Atlantic.

Progress seemed so relentless that many were skeptical of humanity's ability to use science wisely, as seen in ever-more sophisticated weapons of war.[5] This tendency to anti-positivism was relatively strong in the Czech lands (see the narrator's allusion to "the wretchedness of materialism"

---

2. Jahoda-author Bulkin e-mail, May 2021.
3. Manufactured by the Nesselsdorfer-Wagenbau-Fabriks-Gesellschaft A.G. See video at https://www.youtube.com/watch?v=HLwuXnhykUA.
4. Pavel Beneš, "Elegantní jednoplošník Rapid bratří Čiháků—první letadlo české konstrukce."
5. For example, various mid-19th-century innovations improved artillery accuracy, including breech loading, rifling (spiral grooving) of cannon bores, optical targeting, and hydraulic recoil management.

in *The Martians'* final chapter). After all, innovations during World War I had included not only air traffic control and hydrophones but also machine guns and poison gas. Morality seemed unable to keep pace with technology.

Like many of her contemporaries, Procházková hoped that humanity's future would look brighter than its past. In her novella *The Martians*, the red planet hosts a civilization far more advanced than Earth's, socially and technologically—as well as spiritually and in its gender relations. In creating this vision, Procházková became one of the first women in Central Europe to write science fiction and the first to do so in Czech. Within the arc of her national tradition, her ethical framework is distinctive for its esotericism, proto-feminism, progressivism, and pacifism. Her aesthetic strikes the modern reader as not only steampunk but decopunk.

Early Czech Fantastic Literature

Czech science-fiction scholar Ondřej Neff (b. 1945) finds that most nineteenth-century European writers looked askance at science and technology, even in fantastic literature. He observes that even tech-friendly French author Jules Verne (1828–1905) portrayed scientists and inventors "almost exclusively [as] oddballs and grotesque figures or even madmen and criminals."

From its modern beginnings in the early nineteenth century until World War II, Czech fantastic literature rarely depicted fanciful technologies. For decades, gothic fiction remained a staple of popular reading. After the first original Czech gothic short fiction of the 1820s by Jan Hýbl and Jan z Hvězdy, the first Czech fantastic (gothic) novel was *Pekla zplozenci* (Hellspawn; serialized 1853, book 1862) by the actor, author, and Shakespeare/Schiller translator Josef Jiří Kolár (1812–1896). It tells of a young man unjustly condemned to hanging but reprieved by a bolt of lightning that strikes the gallows. He finds shelter with an alchemist, who persuades him to become his subject in an experiment to create immortal beings. The young man's dead mother, once demon-possessed, raises her voice in protest, and the ensuing battle of good and evil leads to the alchemical laboratory's destruction. In the background, historical figures such as Prague-based Habsburg emperor Rudolf II (r. King of Bohemia 1575–1612, Holy Roman Emperor 1576–1612) add local color. When Czech fantastic fiction did begin to incorporate technology, the emphasis was often on its human impact. For example, in "A Hundred Years On" (1841), an early sketch by Jakub Malý (1811–1885) in which technology is sometimes a source of wonder (a printing press that scans copy for errors) but often brings doubtful benefits (phrenological rectification helmets that prevent pernicious character traits in children but are often lethal).

English-language readers may know Czech author Jakub Arbes (1840–1914) for his time-travel tale *Newtonův mozek* (Newton's Brain, 1877) in translation.[6] This work and Arbes's other "romanettos" (short novels) remain grounded in reality even when some fantastic element is suggested. In *Newton's Brain,* a soldier receives Isaac Newton's brain from a museum following a head injury in wartime. He invents a time machine that leads him to realize that human history is nothing but wars and bloodshed. However, all this turns out to have been the narrator's dream.

6. See Jakub Arbes, "Newton's Brain" in bibliography for English translations.

Among other early Czech fantastic works, Neff cites two novels by Svatopluk Čech (1846–1908): *Pravý výlet pana Broučka do Měsíce* (Mr. Brouček's True Journey to the Moon; serialized 1886, book 1887) and *Nový epochální výlet pana Broučka, tentokrát do XV. století* (Mr. Brouček's New Epochal Trip, This Time to the Fifteenth Century; 1889). He frames them as "allegorical grotesques" in the Swiftian mode rather than as modern science fiction. Allegories and utopias constitute much of other European fantastic literature in this period.

Verne's highly popular example inspired a few tentative fantastic works in Czech prior to World War I, for example Karel Hloucha's short-story collection for children *Podivuhodné Jiříčkovo cestování* (Georgie's Remarkable Travels, [1907]). However, the genre became markedly more productive only in the 1920s and 1930s.[7] Czech author Eva Hauserová (1954–2023) characterizes that broader surge as "deeply humanistic" and concerned with maintaining human values amid technological change rather than with fantastic-voyage heroics[8] or "space opera." Neff argues that this humanist focus in Czech fantastic literature is a legacy of World War I, the carnage of which seemed to justify skepticism toward scientific "progress." He finds that outlook in both Karel Čapek (1890–1938), author of the internationally popular play *R.U.R.* (Rossum's Universal Robots; published 1920, Czech premiere 1921),

---

7. In a 1995 study, Czech science-fiction scholar Ivan Adamovič counted zero to two Czech fantasy titles per year from 1861 to 1918, and no double-digit figure until 1918 (Ivan Adamovič, Ondřej Neff, and Jaroslav Olša, Jr., *Slovník*, 262). While more titles have come out of the woodwork since then, this pattern would most likely hold.
8. See Ivan Adamovič and Jaroslav Olša, Jr., "Czech and Slovak SF"; and Eva Hauser[ová], "Science Fiction in the Czech Republic and the Former Czechoslovakia."

and Jan Weiss (1892–1972), author of *Dům o tisíci patrech* (House of a Thousand Floors; serialized 1928, book 1929).[9]

More generally, Neff finds this period's Czech science-fiction writers to be creatively largely isolated as individuals, lacking any sense of community as fantastic writers—and partial to "allegories" reflecting their highly personal visions for the future of humanity. The Czech reading public viewed such "utopian" works as minor curiosities. Westerns and detective stories were more popular. With few exceptions, all known authors of Czech works with fantastic elements prior to World War I were male (see entries for Sofie Podlipská and Amálie Vrbová in the appendix "Women of Speculation").

Women Authors of Speculative Fiction

Women have been vital to fantastic literature from its beginnings. Ann Radcliffe (1764–1823) left a lasting influence on the gothic novel. Mary Wollstonecraft Shelley (1797–1851) is generally credited with starting something new with her novel *Frankenstein, or, the Modern Prometheus* (1818). Jane (Webb) Loudon (1807–1858) deserves mention as the author of the novel *The Mummy! A Tale of the Twenty-Second Century* (1827). Despite a long succession of women's contributions to fantastic writing,[10]

---

9. Čapek's "robots" (he credited his brother Josef with coining the word) have literary precedents in E. T. A. Hoffmann, Edgar Allan Poe, and Herman Melville, but also in the even older golem legend of Prague. *R.U.R.* was quickly translated into French by Hanuš Jelínek (1920) and then into English, though initially heavily edited. As of 2024, Weiss's novel had been translated into 10 languages, including English in 2016 (see bibliography).

10. L. Timmel Duchamp's webpage "Science Fiction and Utopias by Women, 1818–1949: A Chronology" leads off with Shelley.

works by their male counterparts dominate most surveys.

The Central and East European women authors of pre-1945 works cited in their respective country surveys in the *Encyclopedia of Science Fiction* are the Baroness Bertha von Suttner (1843–1914) (Austrian), Thea von Harbou (1888–1954) (German), Marie Grubhofferová (1901–1977) (Czech), and perhaps misleadingly, Margit Kaffka (1880–1918) (Hungarian).[11] In 1905, the Prague-born von Suttner became the first woman to win the Nobel Peace Prize. Like Procházková's *The Martians*, her somewhat fantastic novel *Der Menschheit Hochgedanken, Roman aus der nächsten Zukunft* (When Thoughts Will Soar: A Romance of the Immediate Future, 1911) reimagines women's roles in society and marvels at technology's prospects. It features a passionate young female protagonist and a melodramatic flavor.[12] Von Harbou authored the novel *Metropolis* (1925) as well as the screenplay filmed by her husband Fritz Lang in 1927.[13] In Grubhofferová's *Prázdniny ve hvězdách* (Holiday Among the Stars, 1937), some Earth children aged three to fourteen travel to Venus, become local favorites by slaying an evil prince, and return to Earth with one of their new friends; her *Mezihvězdní piráti* (Interstellar Pirates, 1939) picks up

---

Mary Mark Ockerbloom's "A Celebration of Women Writers: Utopias and Science Fiction by Women" begins with *The Countesse of Mountgomeries Urania* (1621) by Lady Mary Wroth (ca.1586–ca.1640) and *The Blazing World* (1623) by Margaret (Lucas) Cavendish, Duchess of Newcastle (1623–1673).

11. Kaffka is considered Hungary's first major woman writer but was not a fantasist. Her novels *Színek és évek* (Colors and Years, 1912) and *Hangyaboly* (The Ant Heap, 1917) have been translated into English.

12. *When Thoughts Will Soar* is available online in English (see appendix).

13. Jesica Brubaker, "Early Female Authors of Science Fiction/Fantasy"; and Alpers, "Germany."

the story. Among those missing in these articles are the widely translated Russian Vera Ivanovna Kryzhanovskaia (1861–1924), with her pentalogy *Маги* (The Magicians, 1901–16) and other occult works; and the Romanian Olga Caba (1913–1995).

These and other Central and East European women authors of fantastic literature have gone all but unmentioned in English-language surveys of the genre. This edition of *The Martians* therefore includes an initial bibliography of women writers of pre-1950 speculative fiction from the region.

Why were there so few women writing speculative fiction in pre-World War II Central and East Europe? Even where literacy was as widespread as in the Czech lands, women writers were a relative novelty. Even apart from social norms, few women enjoyed the leisure to write fiction. Moreover, women had less access to higher education. Only *Gymnasium* (university-preparatory academy) graduates could apply to enter a university, but there was no girls' *Gymnasium* anywhere in Austria-Hungary until 1890, when feminist poet, librettist, and translator Eliška Krásnohorská (1847–1926) founded the Minerva School in Prague. Nevertheless, early Bohemian women of science included botanist-paleontologist Josefina Kablíková (1787–1863); botanist-entomologist Marie Zdeňka Baborová-Čiháková (1877–1937), the first woman to earn a Ph.D. in the Czech lands; archaeologist Ludmila Matiegková (1889–1960); and pharmacologist Hedwig Langecker (1894–1989). The first woman to earn a medical doctorate from Charles-Ferdinand University in Prague was Anna Horáková (1875–1940) in 1902. Her only predecessors, Anna Bayerová (1852–1924) and Bohuslava Kecková (1854–1911), both received their degrees in

Switzerland. The first woman to practice medicine in Austria-Hungary was Gabriele Possaner (1860–1940)—only after she redefended her Zurich degree in Vienna in 1897.

The fictional women scientists in *The Martians'* chapter "The Feast of Talents" are Lektona, inventor of a videophone; and the perfumer Stemfa. The latter may have been modeled on Coco Chanel, who had created Chanel No. 5 the year before the novella was published. In this chapter, these women are honored alongside their male counterparts, and all of those so honored are motivated by the public good rather than profit. These sketches are consistent with what Neff characterizes as the period's general view of scientists as "essentially romantic" figures battling abstract unknowns.

Spiritualism and Theosophy in Central Europe

Procházková was a self-declared "spirit writer"—although unlike Kryzhanovskaia, her internationally famous contemporary who claimed to channel John Wilmot, Second Earl of Rochester (1647–1680), Procházková did not declare *whose* spirit she was channeling in her books. Nevertheless, the title pages of all her known works include the phrase *psáno medijně* (written by mediumship).[14]

---

14. Other period spirit writers include the American Sara Weiss (*Journeys to the Planet Mars*, 1903) and J. L. Kennon (pseud. of [the American Mabel J. McKean]; *The Planet Mars and Its Inhabitants*, 1922). Another figure of interest is the clairvoyant Swiss Hélène Smith (pseud. of Catherine-Elise Müller, 1861–1929), who claimed to be a reincarnated Indian princess able to communicate with the Martians in their language (see Robert Crossley, *Imagining Mars: A Literary History*).

Similar claims were made by English theosophist Annie Besant (1847–1933) and Scotsman William Sharp (1855–1905).[15]

The pan-European fashion for spiritualism is evident in *The Martians*, for example in Procházková's novel depiction of "celestial dictation," a form of interplanetary communication using "ethereal script."[16] The practice combines the concepts of alchemy, astral projection, Marconi's telegraph, and Edison's phonograph as used for dictation. French author and scientist Camille Flammarion (1842–1925) was a partisan of telepathy and clairvoyance; his novel *Uranie* (Uranus, 1889; German transl. 1894, Czech transl. 1924)[17] ushered in a host of spiritistically

---

Smith was the daughter of a Hungarian merchant. She became famous with the publication of University of Geneva psychology professor Théodore Flournoy's study *Des Indes à la planète Mars* (From India to the Planet Mars, 1900).

15. William F. Halloran, *The Life and Letters of William Sharp and "Fiona Macleod,"* vol. 3, 142–3.

16. *Nebeské diktando* is Procházková's Czech term for "celestial dictation." "Diktando" is a distinctly Latinate early/mid-nineteenth century word for "dictation," in the sense of a schoolhouse exercise. It appears in both Czech and Bohemian-German period texts. It is glossed in an 1849 Czech "abecedary" of foreign terms and occurs twice in Božena Němcová's classic novel *Babička* (Granny, 1855).

See *Harper's Weekly* 32, no. 1642 (June 9, 1888), 415–6 for an illustration of a Victorian-era dictation machine ("Edison's Perfected Phonograph").

The notion that space was filled by ether, through which gravity and electromagnetic signals were transmitted, was eventually abandoned after Einstein's theory of relativity (1905) gained acceptance.

17. Several other Flammarion titles had been translated into Czech prior to *The Martians'* publication, including the novels *Lumen* (1872) in 1905, *Les forces naturelles inconnues* (Unknown Natural Forces, 1907) in [1907], and *Voyages en ballon* (Balloon Journeys, 1881) in 1908, *Stella* (1897) in 1910, as well as the multi-volume study *La mort et son*

colored works on Mars. Whether directly influenced by Flammarion or not, H. G. Wells' *The War of the Worlds* (1898) depicts Martians communicating by telepathy, and Edgar Rice Burroughs has his hero reach Mars via a form of astral projection in *A Princess of Mars* (1912). Procházková's own "celestial dictation" may have been a creative variation on this theme. It also appears to anticipate the "ansible" described in Ursula K. Le Guin's *Hainish Cycle* (1966–).

Other examples of spiritualism's influence in *The Martians* include depictions of communication with the dead (though not by seance but by mail), the influence of unseen forces on the material world (as when the videophones at the aerodrome malfunction), the quasi-occult power of electricity and magnetism, "hexing" via mental suggestion, and the regenerative power of love. The *fin de siècle* fashion for what Canadian cultural studies scholar John Fekete calls "oriental mysticism" was evident in other Central European speculative fiction as well.[18] In truth, mysticism and spiritism were less marginal in this period than they became after World War II.[19]

Interest in mysticism and the paranormal spread rapidly in the period before World War I, extending to spiritism, theosophy, the occult, the paranormal, mediumism, telepathy, hypnosis, somnambulism, reincarnation, and the supernatural in general. That resurgence is often explained

---

mystère (Death and Its Mystery, 1920) in 1921; and not a few others. For a translation of *Uranie* into English, see bibliography. For a partial listing of other Flammarion works and their translations, see Isfdb.org.

18. John Fekete, "Science Fiction in Hungary," 194.

19. Aside from questions of empirical evidence for spiritist phenomena and the exposure of charlatans, the postwar association of Nazism with mysticism likely played a role. For a more recent assessment, see Eric Kurlander, "Between Weimar's Horrors and Hitler's Monsters."

as a reaction to the rapid pace of scientific innovation, although Masonic lodges and various secret societies had long propagated the esoteric arts in Europe and the U.S. Professor of English Robert Crossley also points to the 1877 close approach of Earth and Mars as a catalyst for much new speculation on Mars (as well as interest in astronomy). It was then that Italian astronomer Giovanni Schiaparelli (1855–1910) created the first detailed map of the red planet, complete with "channels" (which *The Martians* helpfully explains).

At the time, many scientists, scholars, and cultural figures of the period shared in this interest. In France, the educator Allan Kardec (1804–1869) founded the Société parisienne des études psychiques (SPES) in 1858; the national Union spirite française (French Spirit Union) followed in 1882. In London, the Society for Psychical Research (SPR) was founded that same year, and its membership included both spiritists and scientists—although few among the latter were outright "partisans" of supernaturalism.[20] An American SPR followed in 1885, and the popular writer-astronomer Percival Lowell (1855–1916) consulted with its leadership.[21] Kryzhanovskaia was married to the head of the St. Petersburg SPR. The French journal *Revue spirite* is replete with references to contacts among such European societies.[22]

Between 1880 and 1910, there was a general revival of occultism in Germany and Austria,[23] where it influenced the ethnic-nationalist Völkish movement. The visionary

20. Crossley, *Imagining Mars*, 129–30.
21. On this point, Crossley cites Lowell's biographer David Strauss.
22. Archived in French at the International Association for the Preservation of Spiritualist and Occult Periodicals (Iapsop.com) and Internet Archive (archive.org).
23. Nicholas Goodrick-Clarke, *The Occult Roots of Nazism*.

educational reformer, philosopher, and author Rudolf Steiner (1861–1925) founded a Theosophical Society in Germany in 1902.[24] He abandoned it within a few years, averse to the growing focus on Indian thought within the movement, and he established the Anthroposophical Society as an alternative. Steiner's teachings led to the creation of the Waldorf educational method. Anthroposophy shares a pedigree with the modern New Age movement.[25]

In the Czech lands, a small theosophical society of about ten adherents took shape in Prague at the end of the 1880s; a larger one, the Český teosofický spolek (Czech Theosophical Association) with about thirty members was started there in 1897. Steiner lectured in Prague twelve times between 1906 and 1924, and he appears to have influenced the direction of the Česká společnost teosofická (Czech Theosophical Society, founded in 1908), which grew from 88 to 171 members by 1914. Steiner appealed directly to Czech national pride: he described the Czech Holy Roman Emperor Karel IV as the last "consecrated" emperor, and he was interested in Habsburg emperor Rudolf II's support for the esoteric arts of alchemy and astrology. The direct influence of Steiner's ideas is seen in the name of the Český antroposofický spolek Studium (the Studium Czech Anthroposophical Association), founded in the mid-1910s and active in independent Czechoslovakia after the war and into at least the 1930s.

The fashion for spiritism spread to Czech cities from the foothills of the Krkonoše (Giant) Mountains in East

---

24. Of note, Steiner began as a Nietzsche scholar (Taylor 2013: 20-21). Especially after Nietzsche's death in 1900 and the subsequent growth in his popular appeal, theosophists liked to claim him as a fellow traveler.
25. Robert Bezděk, "Antroposofie a její vliv na spiritualitu v českém prostředí."

Bohemia, and even "good" society readily partook of seances; however, the authorities might look askance on such enthusiasms, interrogating attendees and "persecuting" lecturers on occultism. Their intervention was inconsistent; at other times, large recurring meetings were held, and spiritist periodicals might be distributed, as scholar Milan Nakonečný writes.[26] There were efforts in 1896 to found the first Czech spiritist association, allegedly to be called the Spiritistická společnost pro psychologická studia (Spiritist Society for Psychological Research), thwarted by Prague police as "dangerous to public health," as one leading spiritist figure, Karel Sezemský, recalled in a 1930 book. Even if that memory may actually relate to the Společnost pro psychická studia (Society for Psychical Studies), its statutes formulated in 1909, spiritism's presence in Central Europe is clear.[27]

At least some scientists sought to integrate spiritist ideas into their research. Many of Carl Jung's writings in the emerging field of psychoanalysis are difficult to disentangle from occult studies,[28] even if his modern-day acolytes insist he was no mystic. The French astronomer Flammarion's works combined astronomy and parapsychology. In a 1900 letter to his countryman, the composer Saint-Saëns, the author asserted that "clairvoyance [...] is *incontestable*."[29] Flammarion was a member of the SPES as a teenager and later the president of the international SPR.

Many artists also felt the lure of spiritism. The

---

26. Milan Nakonečný, *Novodobý český hermetismus* (2nd ed.), 45.

27. Andrea Hudáková, *Organizace československého spiritistického hnutí*, 49–50.

28. See Júlia Gyimesi, "The Problem of Demarcation: Psychoanalysis and the Occult."

29. Crossley, *Imagining Mars*, 130 (emphasis in original), citing Flammarion's reproduction of the letter in his *Houses* (see bibliography).

Russian composer Stravinsky denounced "scientism" and bureaucracy as modern evils inimical to "the Russian soul" (mythologized by many of Stravinsky's contemporaries).[30] His fellow Russian, the author Helena Blavatsky (1831–1891), emigrated to the United States and founded the Theosophical Society in New York in 1875. Among other things, Blavatsky taught that an ancient and mysterious fraternity of spiritual "Masters" was scattered across the world. The Society grew to international prominence and claimed not a few "Masters" among its devotees, including the painters Kandinsky and Mondrian, the poet Yeats, the composer Scriabin, and inventor Thomas Edison——in whose phonograph Procházková imagined her Martians hearing voices from the beyond.

Theosophy also assigned particular significance to colors, a scheme explored in the handbook *Thought-Forms* (1905) by Blavatsky's close collaborator Annie Besant (1847–1933).[31] Maria Carlson finds this scheme reflected in Russian writer Andrei Belyi's novel *Петербург* (Petersburg, 1912),[32] and it may be partially reflected in *The Martians*: yellow (pure intellect in Besant's scheme) is the color of the bread Igo Phenomén serves the scientists who dine with him. Jealous Lerk's eyes, feckless Iva's eyebrows, and the bereaved Cara's pearls are all black (anger); Iva's lips are red (malice) as she meets Phenomén for a fatal assignation. However, green does not convey foreboding as in either *Thought-Forms* or *Petersburg*. Besant's volume appeared in German translation in 1908, well before *The Martians'*

30. See Orlando Figes, *Natasha's Dance: A Cultural History of Russia*, ch. 4.

31. *On color in Petersburg*, see also Christine D. Tomei, "On the Function of Light and Color in Andrej Belyj's *Petersburg*: Green and Twilight."

32. See Maria Carlson, "Fashionable Occultism."

publication, and was possibly accessible to Procházková. Her familiarity with this internationally popular theosophist work is plausible.

Theosophical and anthroposophical ideas were thus available to authors in Prague, and this was reflected in both Czech- and German-language local literature. The life and works of banker, translator, and writer Gustav Meyrink (1868–1932), author of the novel *Der Golem* (The Golem, 1915), based on a Prague Jewish legend, resonate with esoteric and theosophical concepts. Along with the author and critic Jiří Karásek ze Lvovic (1871–1951) and author Julius Zeyer (1841–1901),[33] Meyrink was linked to the Christian-esotericist Martinist order in Prague,[34] as was author Emanuel Lešehrad[35] (1877–1955). Works by author and journalist Karel Matěj Čapek-Chod (1860–1927)—not to be confused with the works of Karel Čapek—including the novels *Antonín Vondrejc* (1915) and *Jindrové* (The Henrys, 1921) reflect contemporary interest in Indian thought. His novel *Turbina* (The Turbine, 1916) touches on the notion of extraterrestrial forces on human events—as always for this writer, with a tongue-in-cheek approach. The diaries of Franz Kafka (1883–1924) record a meeting with Steiner, whom he asked for advice on his own

---

33. British Bohemist Robert Pynsent finds theosophy the "basis" to Zeyer's short story "Opálová miska" (The Opal Bowl, 1878) (Robert Pynsent, *Julius Zeyer: The Path to Decadence*; see related footnote to *The Martians* chapter "The Song of Máv"). Karásek and Lešehrad later edited a journal of the occult (see below). For both, the appeal of speculative thought overlapped with its aesthetic possibilities.
34. David Plass, "Historie Martinistického řádu v Čechách," 24–6.
35. Karásek, Lešehrad, and fellow author Josef Šimánek (1883–1959) were not only all early Czech fantasists but Decadents associated with the literary journal *Moderní revue* (1894–1925) (Cyril Simsa, "Josef Šimánek (1883–1959): Czech Pagan Fantasist").

emerging interest in theosophy and anthroposophy. Kafka ultimately abandoned that pursuit, concerned that too deep an involvement would interfere with his writing and his employment. At any rate, such ideas transcended national boundaries, there were civil-society organizations to bring the like-minded together even in Bohemia, and these ideas found expression in literature—as in Procházková's novella *The Martians*.

Procházková: Profile, Publishers, and Predilections

Czech science-fiction encyclopedist Ivan Adamovič summarizes *The Martians* as a love triangle involving two scientists and a florist,

> all of them living on Mars. The focus of the book is [...] Martian civilization, which [...] is not a rigid Utopia but a dynamic, technically advanced society that values labor and courage. The book is written in lovely, poetic language that, unlike what is found in other Czech contemporary works, is not especially dated.[36]

The novella was published in an inexpensive chapbook format common for popular reading (usually an adventure story without literary pretensions). The format likely resembled that of the *Groschenhefte* (saddle-stapled booklets) found in both Germany and the U.S. from the turn of the century onward, for example the series *Aus dem Reiche der Phantasie* (From the Realms of Imagination, 1901) by Robert Kraft (1869–1916).

Procházková herself remains something of a mystery, although recent research has brought additional

36. Adamovič, Neff, and Olša, Jr., *Slovník*, 186.

biographical detail to light.[37] She was born in 1878.[38] A native and lifelong resident of Roztoky near Prague, Emilie née Nováková married František Procházka, an outgoing railway conductor. Before or during the 1910s, her enthusiasm for spiritism attracted the notice of Karel Sezemský (see above) from Nová Paka in East Bohemia, since he published her first known work in 1917,[39] when she was 39. Her other known works are the ambitious hexalogy *V koloběhu světů* (As Worlds Circulate, 1920–2) and *The Martians.* Their publication history takes us through some of the layers of the spiritism fashion in Prague itself.

Procházková wrote both works at a triumphant time in Czech history. The 300-year-old Habsburg Monarchy had fallen. As Czechoslovakia became independent in 1918, change was in the air. Looking back about ten years afterward, attorney František Čeřovský recalled a sense of *osvobozovací ideologie* (liberation ideology) and *liberálně vyčkávací stanovisko* (expectations of liberalization).[40] Yet as many newly-wealthy residents of Prague built summer villas in her hometown of Roztoky,[41] Procházková may have questioned whether Czech society had lost sight of its spiritual priorities.

---

37. See, in particular, Ivan Adamovič, "Psaní jako kosmická telegrafie. Po stopách první ženské autorky české fantastiky."
38. Jaromír Kozák, *Spiritismus: zapomenutá významná kapitola českých dějin,* 319, 652. Kozák notes a special performance of G. B. Shaw's play *Saint Joan* (1923) at the Municipal Theater in Royal Vinohrady (today the Vinohrady Theater) for the benefit of the Czechoslovak Spiritualist Society (Obec československých spiritistů) on June 13, 1948. Best wishes for Procházková's seventieth birthday were read from the stage during the principal intermission.
39. Her first known work is *Mysterie života: pouť ducha říší astrální* (The Mystery of Life: A Spirit's Journey Through the Astral Realm, 1917).
40. Jan Seidl et al., *Od žaláře k oltáři,* 35–7.
41. Anonymous, "Historie města."

The first three volumes of the hexalogy were published under the imprint of the Czech Theosophical Society. The Society was housed in Prague's famed Lucerna complex near Wenceslas Square. The building belonged to a prominent Society member: construction entrepreneur and arts patron Vácslav Havel (1861–1921), grandfather of playwright and president Václav Havel (1936–2011). The head of the Society introduced Procházková to the elder Havel, who conferred with extraterrestrials with the help of mediums[42]—and was clearly captivated by Procházková's writing. Signing himself "Atom,"[43] Havel contributed the foreword to volume one of *As Worlds Circulate: Comtesa Ester* (Countess Esther, 1920). Volume two, *Róza, pokračování Komtesy Ester* (Rosa, A Sequel to Countess Esther) was issued the same year. In Procházková's "chaste" way, deeply imbued with Christian and Indian mysticism, as Adamovič notes, carnal relations between men and women are portrayed either as an undesirable form of procreation or in spiritually idealized terms. The Countess Esther desires a child but wants no male to take part in its conception. Rosa, who loves both the male Rij and Esther, enters into Rij's incarnated body with her soul and then becomes Esther's wife.[44]

After Havel's death in 1921, the narrative shifts into more fantastic territory. The next two parts of the series are named *Uran* (Uranus I–II), perhaps recalling the title of Flammarion's *Uranie* (1889). Per Adamovič's summary, "Uranus is [portrayed as] a planet where the souls of some

---

42. Adamovič, "Psaní."

43. As confirmed by contemporary letters and later by Vácslav's son Ivan (Martin C. Putna, *Václav Havel*, 34–5).

44. Adamovič, "Psaní"; see also below on Otto Weininger's concept of "bisexuality."

individuals can be reincarnated after death."[45] The final part then takes place in wartime Russia, where revolutionaries seek to become prophets and spiritual leaders for a new world.

Uranus II was followed by *V moři plamenů* (In a Sea of Flames) and *Země ohně (Saturn)* (Land of Fire [Saturn], published in a single binding in 1922). These last three volumes were brought out by Zmatlík and Palička (whose company logo, an owl, represents esoteric knowledge). The press was headed by Jan Zmatlík (1869–aft. 1945), who brought his sons into the firm by the mid-1920s. As a sideline, Jan sold the cure-all medicine Eukalyptin,[46] went on to lecture for the local spiritualist society Průkopník (Pioneer) in the 1930s, and was attached to a Martinist lodge in Prague.[47]

Zmatlík and Palička brought out an eclectic mix of about 750 titles from 1908 to 1948 as well as the journal *Okultní a spiritualistická revue* (Occult and Spiritualist Revue, 1921–4), edited by Karásek and Lešehrad in its final two years. The titles consisted of both translations and original Czech works on spiritism, with individual entries on topics such as psychokinesis (mind over matter) and a range of Indian thought. Its 1922 catalog included volumes by two disciples of the nineteenth-century Indian mystic Ramakrishna: Swami Abhedananda (1866–1939), head of the Vedanta Society of New York from 1897 onward; and Swami Vivekananda (1863–1902), <u>instrumental</u> in Hinduism's late-nineteenth-century

45. Adamovič, Neff, and Olša, Jr., *Slovník*, 185–6.

46. Eucalyptus oil has historically been used as a natural remedy to fight colds.

47. See Aleš Zach, "Zmatlík a Palička," which lists many of the authors published by the press. For more on Průkopník, see Hudáková, 43. For more on Martinism in the Czech lands, see Plass.

recognition in the West as a major world religion. There was also a work by Brahma Mahatma Arsaja, a proponent of Raja (mind-body) yoga. Among the translations were *A Strange Story* (1862) ("a novel of black magic") by Edward George Bulwer-Lytton (1803–1873), an English writer[48] and Whig politician; Arthur Conan Doyle's *The Mystery of Cloomber* (1888); and works by Prentice Mulford (1834–1891), a California writer instrumental in the New Thought movement.

Zmatlík and Palička were far from the only Czech publishers dealing in spiritistic works, attesting to the appetites of the reading public. To name only a few others, Sfinx (where Lešehrad worked as an editor) published numerous titles in the same vein, as did the Děčín bookseller O. Pyšvejc via his press in Prague.[49] Hejda and Tuček published several translations by Flammarion and Annie Besant, and Procházková's first known work was published by Karel Sezemský in Nová Paka.[50] Advances in communications, transport, and printing technology greatly expanded publishing in Central Europe from the late nineteenth century through the *fin de siècle* period.[51] In the Czech lands, the end of Habsburg-era censorship also contributed.

---

48. The opening line of Bulwer-Lytton's *Paul Clifford* (1830) has become a totem for egregious prose: "It was a dark and stormy night."
49. Among Pyšvejc's titles is *Veliké tajemství, čili, odhalený okultismus* (The Great Mystery, or Occultism Revealed, 1922), translated from Eliphas Lévi's French text.
50. Adamovič notes one Procházková manuscript (*Pan Řehoř*) that appears to be lost. He also speculates that the 1926 Sezemský title *Jeanne d´Arc: Panna Orleánská* (Jeanne d'Arc: The Maid of Orléans) by Anna Vavřínová may have been written by Procházková under a pseudonym (Adamovič, "Psaní").
51. Sandra Mayer, *Oscar Wilde in Vienna*, 51.

Amid this ferment, *The Martians* stands out not only as an early example of Central European science fiction, pre-World War II spiritist literature, and proto-feminism; it also effectively captures a generational vision of technological and moral progress as imagined by a lively and questioning mind. There is "earnest moralizing," to be sure, frequently italicized in the text lest we miss it, but that does not bury the plot. As science fiction, the work portrays a future that its earnest author presented as plausible. On the one hand, Procházková's vision is speculative: she imagines miracle-working lamps, video telephones, individualized perfumes, and women's full legal equality, along with electric-powered cars, trains, typewriters, and precision aircraft-guidance systems.

On the other hand, the novella reflects how its author likely perceived her own time: new opportunities for women's economic and emotional independence, even as "coquetry" (*koketerie*) remained an essential strategy to manage relations with men; women's role in inspiring men to greater ambition; men's view of women as interchangeable; men's preference for women who are virtuous; and the tendency, even by a "good," desirable man, to infantilize a woman. Yet it would also seem to reflect the contemporary idea expressed in Otto Weininger's *Geschlecht und Charakter* (Sex and Character, 1903) that human beings are "bisexual," containing the essence of both genders—with the corollary that women are essential to guiding men's ambition.[52] Clothing styles

---

52. This idea is equally implicit in von Suttner's *When Thoughts Will Soar*. Of note, von Suttner's autobiography came out in Czech in 1896. See Joanna Czaplińska, "Does Czech Science Fiction Have a (Feminine) Gender" on Weininger's applicability to second-wave Czech feminist science fiction.

on Procházková's Mars look charmingly dated: the chic Iva wears netting over her brow and long skirts with a train to drape over one elbow; the men wear hats that they doff in salute.

Individuals show characteristics that are "natural" to their ethnicity or nationality, and there is even a certain unquestioned xenophobia: the narrator tells Earthlings that Mars' proud and fiery Uguls are "rather like your Germans," its milder Lopuses by implication more "like" the Czechs. The "Homays" Lerk and Máv are conscious of other Martians' dislike of them because of their origins. Iva's aristocratic nemesis Igo Phenomén, however, is above these nationalistic differences.

The author's vision also reflects the mystery and wonder of recent inventions (electricity, the airplane, the light bulb, the automobile) and the popular appeal of esoteric thought in her day. Martian engineer Astor chides his Earth counterparts for neglecting the "spiritual path" in their technological efforts to contact his world. While the Martians of this novella are clearly idealized in their morality and technology, they cohabit the author's era, living at the time of Earth's World War I (see the chapter "Zagara City").

The novella's most striking character may well be the sinister, debonair nobleman Igo Phenomén, with his evil eye that wilts flowers at a glance and his predatory taste for lovely Martian women. (Our doubly unfortunate protagonist is both a florist *and* a lovely Martian woman.) Phenomén is a Martian government official, a prominent patron of the sciences, and a foreigner from a different part of Mars. His evil eye can be resisted only by "strong will" and countered by powers of mental suggestion—and possibly by Astor's restorative violet lamp.

As a villain, Phenomén seems to come straight out of central casting for an early Universal Studios horror film. At one point he is even described as "like a vampire" (*jako upír*)—and indeed, he has the power to drain his victims of their spirit. While Phenomén is drawn partly from European vampire lore,[53] he also evokes the recent novel *Dracula* (1897) by Irish writer Bram Stoker (1847–1912) in that he is an aristocrat. He seems to anticipate Bela Lugosi's 1927 debut on Broadway as Count Dracula, a role Lugosi then vividly reprised on film for Universal in 1931. For the modern reader, this is much of the fun of *The Martians*, even if unintentional.

The chapter "The Dignity of Labor" portrays a civilization driven by ideals of technology, progress, ambition, the trans-formation of nature, and universal labor. In this vision, those who "can no longer work" may take their own lives voluntarily, and those who refuse to work are forced into public servitude—a jarringly authoritarian prescription. The novel's vision of applied engineering also reflects early twentieth-century obliviousness to its environmental impact; societies were focused instead on the possibilities of science, labor, and can-do to transform the landscape.

The Martians' political leftism reflects its time. It was published when democratic Czechoslovakia had both a strong social-democratic party and a strengthening

---

53. As witch trials wound down at the end of the 17th century, Europe was roiled by reports from various territories that incorruptible corpses were rising from their graves in the night to drink the blood of the living. The reports came "mainly from the East, from Hungary, Transylvania, the Balkans, [and] Poland, but also from Bohemia and Moravia, somewhat less often from Germany" (Karel Krejčí, *Česká literatura a kulturní proudy evropské*, 33–4).

communist one.[54] The latter was founded in 1921 and belonged to the Comintern or Third International. The ideology of that Soviet-dominated group, established in Moscow in 1919, hardened considerably at its second congress in 1920. Soviet republics had briefly taken hold in neighboring Bavaria, Hungary, and southeastern Slovakia in 1919. In 1921, Russia's own Bolsheviks grew more confident as they gained the upper hand in the post-revolutionary civil war. In Procházková's day, the Communist Party of Czechoslovakia was in the grip of a virulent dogmatism.

On Europe's contemporary "revolutionary scene," as Erica Lagalisse finds, interest in mysticism was widespread,[55] though it was actively discouraged by party orthodoxy after World War II. While *The Martians*' forced-labor brigades and "voluntary" suicides for unproductive workers (see the chapter "The Dignity of Labor") seem eerie harbingers of post-war authoritarianism,[56] the war-weary, even pacifist tone of the chapter "Zagara City" suggests a less uncompromising commitment to victory than the Comintern's. In the end, *The Martians* is more focused on innovation and the harnessing of spiritist forces than politics.

54. The Czechoslovak Social Democratic Workers' Party won 25.7 percent of the votes in the country's first elections in 1920, becoming the largest party in parliament. The communists opposed the bourgeois republic and did not take part in elections until 1925, when they won 12.86 percent and support for the socialists plunged to 8.88 percent.
55. "Socialism and occultism developed in complementary (as well as dialectical) fashion during the 19th century" (Erica Lagalisse, *Occult Features of Anarchism*, 309).
56. "The symbiosis of Blavatsky's Theosophy with eugenics and the association of occult narratives [...] with the rise of fascism [...] are often pointed out" (Lagalisse, 310); but see also Kurlander, "Between Weimar's Horrors and Hitler's Monsters."

Mars in Literature: A Brief Survey

In this period, literary imaginations were roused by Percival Lowell's popular if mistaken images of Mars as both irrigated (*Mars and Its Canals*, 1906)[57] and inhabited (*Mars as the Abode of Life*, 1909). As context to the creation of Procházková's *The Martians*, this section briefly surveys Euro-American Mars-themed fiction, focusing on East-Central Europe, and then takes a short look at Moon-themed fiction. The influence of Kurd Laßwitz's *Auf zwei Planeten* (On Two Planets, 1897) will be addressed afterward.

Fictional journeys to Mars go back at least to U.S. author and businessman Benjamin F. Field (1806–1887), who penned *A Narrative of the Travels and Adventures of Paul Aermont among the Planets* (1873) under the pseudonym Paul Aermont—the mode of travel being a balloon. In the period to World War I, Mars-themed works by U.S., British, and Irish authors often depicted utopian civilizations on the red planet or the "advanced" perspective of Martian visitors to the big blue marble. Mars hosted a socialist Utopia in *Красная звезда* (Red Star, 1908) by Russian author Aleksandr Bogdanov (1873–1928). In Czech fantastic fiction, the novel *Rusové na Martu* (Russians on Mars, 1909) by Metod Suchdolský (1878–1948) portrays an expedition to Earth by benevolent Martians, who abduct two Russian scientists in order to study the mysteries of love and reproduction. In the self-published novel *Slováci v stratosfére* (Slovaks in the Stratosphere, 1936) by Slovak author Samuel Dežo Turčan (1899–1967), balloon-borne

---

57. Lowell and others were influenced by a mistranslation of Schiaparelli's term *canali* ("channels; grooves") as "canals" (Kyle Chayka, "A Short History of Martian Canals and Mars Fever"). Procházková's Martian bridges offer an alternative explanation.

spacefarers discover a Mars divided into male and female hemispheres; a comic narrative alternates with disquisitions on the development of the universe.[58]

The distant planet in the novel *Végnapok* (Last Days, 1847) by Hungarian author Miklós Jósika (1794–1865) remains unnamed but hosts a familiar, futuristic utopian vision.[59] Jósika's compatriot Frigyes Karinthy devised the satirical allegory *Utazás Faremidóba* (Journey to Faremido, 1916)—the planet's name comes from solfège. Both it and its sequel *Capillária* (1921) are likewise set on an imaginary planet; both play off of the Gulliver story.[60] Neither is the planet named in *Мы* (We; written 1920–1, first published 1924 in English), the futuristic dystopia by Evgenii Zamyatin (1884–1937).

Yet few works not written in one of Europe's major languages gained an international audience. For a regional work that exerted a "substantial influence" on European fantastic fiction, encyclopedist Robert K. J. Killheffer and his colleagues point to *Auf zwei Planeten* (*On Two Planets*, 1897) by German author and science historian Kurd Laßwitz's (1848–1910).[61] Laßwitz's novel was a landmark work in its depiction of interplanetary travel based on futuristic science. In depicting Martians landing in the Arctic and battling the Royal Navy, it also imagines a clash between Earth's and Mars's cultures.[62] *On Two Planets*

58. Ondrej Herec and Miloš Ferko, *Slovenská fantastika do roku 2000*, 11–2.

59. Fekete, "Science Fiction in Hungary," 193.

60. Translated into English by Paul Tabori as *Voyage to Faremido* and *Capillaria* (New York: Living Books, 1966).

61. Robert K. J. Killheffer et al, "Mars."

62. On German proto-science fiction in this period, see Hans Joachim Alpers, "Germany"; Fischer, *The Empire Strikes Out*; and SF2 Concatenation, "German Science Fiction up to 1945."

presented a significantly more elaborate vision of Martian civilization than previous works, as well as a fairly benign invasion scenario.

The novel happened to appear the same year as H. G. Wells' Mars-themed story "The Crystal Egg" and his novel *War of the Worlds*; Killheffer observes that Wells' Martians are distinctly hostile in comparison to Laßwitz's (or those of other Central European writers).

In the same period, the French-British cartoonist and *Punch* illustrator George du Maurier (1834–1896) combined the Mars theme with the paranormal in *The Martian* (1897). Edgar Rice Burroughs went on to contribute the space romance *A Princess of Mars* (1912) and its sequels.

Whether on Mars or any other theme, women authors are absent from most national surveys of fantastic literature in East and Central Europe. In English-language fantastic literature, blogger L. Timmel Duchamp cites four Mars-themed works by women from this period, while Mary Mark Ockerbloom lists five. Hungarian author Lola Kosáryné Réz's unpublished *Kampa Daria naplója* (The Diary of Daria Kampa, 1932–49) deserves mention here though, like Jósika's and Karinthy's entries, it is set on fictional planets (see appendix).

Given that the "Mars craze" coincided with the late-nineteenth-century expansion of European publishing, there are comparatively fewer of the earlier works that staged their utopian speculations on the Moon. Histories may mention the ancient Greek author, advocate, and traveler Lucian of Samosata (125–aft. 180 CE).[63] The novel *Somnium* (The Dream, 1608; published 1634) by astronomer Johannes

---

63. Lucian's depiction of a high lunar civilization of three-headed vultures was an allegory that parodied the unlikely travel tales of his past and present.

Kepler (1571–1630), written during the author's lengthy sojourn in Prague, describes the narrator's dream of a boy named Duracotes, whose mother can summon demons capable of describing the lunar orbit and of transporting humans to the Moon. The details are grounded in scientific observations made by Kepler, who formulated the laws of planetary motion.[64] Later tales include the first part of *L'autre monde* (The Other World, 1657) by Cyrano de Bergerac (1619–1655), *The Consolidator* (1705) by Daniel Defoe (ca.1660–1731), and the tongue-in-cheek tale "Unparalleled Adventure of One Hans Pfaall" (1835; revised 1840) by Edgar Allan Poe (1809–1849).[65]

In the nineteenth and twentieth centuries, the Moon became "less fashionable" as a setting for fictional societies,[66] although there were still such significant entries as *Trylogia księżycowa* (The Lunar Trilogy, 1901–11) by Polish writer Jerzy Żuławski (1874–1915).[67] In Central and East European fantastic writing, the Moon was as convenient a setting for political and social allegory as Mars later became. Before Svatopluk Čech's Brouček novels in the 1880s (see above), the Hungarian Ferenc Ney (1814–1889) published his *Utazás a holdba* (Journey to the Moon, 1836), a utopian work that is partly a satire of the pre-1848 political order; the Hungarian-speaking Moon-dwellers are friendly hosts, live in a well-organized society,

---

64. Following several published editions, the Somnium Project ("Kepler's *Somnium* Retweeted") has been sharing a new English translation by Tom Metcalfe.

65. Poe's original title in 1835 was "Hans Phaall—A Tale."

66. Brian Stableford and David Langford. "Moon."

67. Filmed as *Na srebrnym globie* (On the Silver Globe, 1988) by Andrzej Żuławski (see Cultura.pl, "Andrzej Żuławski, 22.11.1940–17.02.2016"), its title taken from the name of Jerzy's first volume. The trilogy is available in a 2021 English translation by Elzbieta Morgan.

and use the advanced techniques of electricity and steam for power.[68] The Slovak novel *Hviezdoveda, alebo, Životopis Krutohlava, čo na Zemi, okolo Mesiaca a Slnka skúsil a čo o obežniciach, vlasaticiach, pôvode a konci sveta vedel* (Star-Science, or the Biography of Krutohlav, What He Experienced on Earth, Around the Moon and the Sun, and What He Knew About Orbits, Comets, [and] the Origin and the End of the World, 1856)[69] by the polymath and founder of Slovak "science fiction" Gustáv Mauricius Reuss (1818–1861) envisioned a trip to the Moon in a Slovak-built, gunpowder-powered balloon seven years before Jules Verne's *Cinq semaines en ballon* (Five Weeks in a Balloon, 1863). However, Reuss's work was not published until 1984, and in form, it "stands between a novel and a fictionalized treatise on astronomy."[70] The Hungarian novel *Repülőgéppel a Holdba* (By Airplane to the Moon, 1899) by István Makay (1870–1935) dispenses with allegory to construct a Verne-inspired technical fantasy. Back on the Czech scene, the novel *Luňan Hvězdomír Blankytný Broučkův host v Praze roku 1891* (The Moon-Dweller Hvězdomír Blankytný [Starman Azure], Brouček's Guest in Prague in 1891; published 1892) by František Josef Studnička is a parody of Čech's allegory rather than an attempt to imagine a plausible alternative reality.

Stableford and Langford cite numerous other works from the 1880s onward that present the Moon not as the setting for a Utopia or social satire but as "a place of

68. See Fekete, "Science Fiction in Hungary."
69. Transl. as *The Science of the Stars* by David Short (London: Jantar, 2024).
70. Herec and Ferko, *Slovenská fantastika*, 9. Also note the likely Verne-inspired work *Výskumy z mesiaca* (Explorations of the Moon, 1893), a politically colored response to Hungary's millennial celebrations by Slovak writer Anton Emanuel Timko (1843–1903).

ultimate desolation where life is extinct." As space travel looked increasingly plausible in the mid-twentieth century, the Moon's resources became a focus of Moon fiction. In Slovak Samo Tokeš's novella *Dobyvatelia Mesiaca* (Conquerors of the Moon, 1948), the lunar setting becomes the backdrop for a twenty-first-century clash between European and Asian nations in competition for supplies of "lunium," an energy-rich element. In Procházková's day, however, speculation about Martian life and civilization was generally more common.

Still other works in the collective Central European fantastic canon ventured to the North Pole: the popular Hungarian author Mór Jókai's (1825–1904) *Egész az Északi pólusig* (All the Way to the North Pole, 1876), Laßwitz's 1897 *On Two Planets*), and the Slovak Ján Kresánek-Ladčan's (1919–1990) *Za nami púšť: Utopistický pribeh o atomovej bombe* (The Desert Behind Us: A Utopian Tale About the Atom Bomb, 1947) are all contributions to the sub-genre of polar fantasy—with corresponding categories for the Amazon, the desert, and the bottom of the sea,[71] and any of these might likewise serve equally well as the setting for an imagined alternative technological or social order, or a futuristic cautionary tale. Ockerbloom finds nine Moon-themed utopian and science-fiction works by women authors up to 1945, including one from the seventeenth century, as well as von Harbou's *Frau im Mond* (The Woman in the Moon, 1928). Additional East-Central European entries would include works by the Countess Fanny von Bernstorff and the short story "Náměsíčná" (The Sleepwalker, 1903) by Czech author Sofie Podlipská.

---

71. See Mór Jókai's "Oceánia" (1856), transl. into English by R. Nisbet Bain as "The City of the Beast" in the collection *Tales from Jókai*.

Procházková's Influences and Legacy

To summarize Procházková's potential influences, it is most clear that she was familiar with contemporary literature on spiritism and theosophy. By the 1910s, Bohemia had developed a lively spiritist scene, with periodicals, publishers, and public meetings. Her own Czech publisher had brought out a translation of Blavatsky's *The Voice of the Silence: Being Chosen Fragments from the Book of the Golden Precepts* (1889) prior to *The Martians'* publication. A volume of Besant's teachings (*The Ancient Wisdom*) had also been published in Czech in 1920, and several of Besant's works had been translated into German[72]—which Procházková likely read, given her life circumstances.

Among potential literary influences, Flammarion's novel *Uranus* (1889) was already available in German and had, in any event, begun to inspire similar fiction. Laßwitz's *On Two Planets* appeared in Czech in 1904. It seems safe to assume that Procházková had been exposed to at least some of her fellow spiritist Flammarion's works, several of them available in Czech prior to the publication of *The Martians*. Prior to the publication of *The Martians*, the idea of Marconian telegraphy or a telephone to Mars did appear in the crude farce "Marconiho telefon s Marsem" (Marconi's Telephone with Mars, 1920) by Czech writer Josefina Nyklesová-Bukovanská (1888–1954).

It is conceivable that Procházková had at least indirect knowledge of Żuławski's or du Maurier's titles. Yet during her school-age years, there was no *Gymnasium* for girls anywhere in Austria-Hungary, only more basic options; so it seems unlikely that she received a thorough grounding in any European language beyond German, although this is a

72. See holdings of Deutsche National Bibliothek at dnb.de.

supposition. Moreover, in her known published works, her interests never strayed far from spiritualism. It hardly seems possible that she did not know of Besant, Flammarion, and Blavatsky.

As a fantastic work with a scientific-technological focus, an imagined civilization on another planet, and presumption of plausibility, *The Martians* makes Procházková arguably the first known Czech woman to write what is now called science fiction. Indeed, she appears to be one of the first in continental Europe to write such a work.[73] In the decades to come, the "fad for alien abduction" would triumph and the benign "man from Mars" give way to "extraterrestrial kidnappers," at least in Anglo-American science fiction.[74] With its broadly humanistic vision, *The Martians* imagines a less hostile unknown, informed by technology, spiritism, and proto-feminism. It constitutes a significant early contribution to science fiction by women.

73. Procházková's only potential antecedent in Czech speculative literature would seem to be Jiří Sumín (pseud. of Amálie Vrbová, 1864–1936). Sumín wrote several short stories with elements of folk magic and superstition (a devil, witch, or contact with the dead). Yet there is no scientific or interplanetary dimension in them; they are not science fiction. Nyklesová-Bukovanská's short prose pieces, written for humor periodicals, are framed as farces. Outside continental Europe, the gender of the anonymous author of *Politics and Life on Mars*, published in London in 1883, is not known. Killheffer suggests that it reflects a "nascent feminism."
74. Crossley, *Imagining Mars*, 144.

In translating this text, I have attempted to preserve the author's modern yet slightly mannered prose, with some inspiration from Edgar Rice Burroughs and H. P. Lovecraft. I have also sought to preserve her essential defamiliarization strategies through spellings such as "aeroplane."

My particular thanks to Ivan Adamovič for rediscovering the work and his subsequent research on Emilie Procházková; and to Melvyn Clarke for both suggesting *The Martians* as a work to translate and commenting on an entire initial draft. I am also indebted to the late Eva Hauserová, to Tony Mileman, Jaroslav Olša, Jr., Garry Richards, Endre Sebők, and Cyril Simsa, who gave helpful suggestions and feedback on this introduction. Any errors here or in the translation are strictly my own responsibility.

This translation is dedicated to the young physicist Isaac Ehle.

—*Carleton Bulkin*

ROMÁNOVÁ OKULTNÍ KNIHOVNA ŠŤASTNÝCH LIDÍ

SVAZEK 3.

E. PROCHÁZKOVÁ:

MARŤANÉ

PSÁNO MEDIJNĚ

ROMÁN

Nakladatelství ZMATLÍK A PALICKA, knihkupectví
PRAHA - LETNÁ.

NAKLADATELSTVÍ · ZMATLÍK A PALIČKA · KNIHKUPECTVÍ PRAHA-LETNÁ.

The Martians

A Missive from Mars

Thousands of eyes and hearts have turned to the familiar planet of Mars. There have been and shall be attempts to establish contact with its inhabitants by wireless telegraphy, light signals, and telepathy, as well as atmospheric disturbances. This shall be the very latest attempt; it may be a poor method and a precarious one, but it is finely calculated.

Your scientists, however, neglect the ever so reliable *spiritual path*. It can vault across the unfathomable abysses of the Universe with ease, needing only a firm will to sustain it.

The pathways between the worlds are free, unbounded. You must join with the Spirits of these spaces, yet you must be at the same time free, unfettered, unburdened by politics, chauvinism, business interests, and the pursuit of profit. Not one of your scientists or researchers knows such freedom, and I therefore cannot dictate my work to any of them.

And so I give it to you.

Take pride in this trophy, which shall one day be placed on your grave like a palm of victory.[1]

—Astor

---

1. Cf. Revelation 7:9.

Friends

"**C**anals!—How ridiculous!—They have no other name for our magnificent works. I've heard this word a hundred times, but I couldn't tell you what is meant or understood by it. Canals and again, *canals!*" The copper wires crackled, and a brass knob fell and dropped on the floor with a thud. The young man glanced at it with the same contempt as his tone held when he turned to his companion.

"Why let that bother you? … They're not advanced enough to understand our work yet. Who could tell them otherwise when they might as well all be asleep? And if our signals wake them from their slumbers and their indifference, they'll never believe in anything again. Send them an ambassador … and they'll laugh at him or put him to the torch.…"

"Surely they're not still torturing their own kind with such a brutal form of killing!" the other grumbled in reply.

"They'll find some other way to kill them, one far more searing: *scorn.*… You'd have to find some heroic soul to do it, someone impartial and free in spirit who neither fears the criticism of scientists nor is daunted by mathematics," advised the first, as he nudged the large globe on the table before him.

"But how, and to which?"

"How? By dictation! Look at my device here. Use it to record your instructions; you know its capabilities, after all," urged the other, and he set the globe spinning rapidly. It whirled upon its thin copper rod, spinning so fast that the sheets of thin paper on the tabletop were gently aflutter….

"Do you think it's possible, by sheer will, to dictate a message to someone from another world, of a different constitution? … I've seen and done all sorts of things, but I wouldn't think this possible. There are various laws I have to consider here…."

"Well, break them, then!" said the other, rising abruptly. His tall, broad-shouldered frame nearly filled the small room where this enigmatic conversation had taken place. His large black eyes bored into his companion's face, which stared back at him in surprise and consternation. He seemed to hesitate, to lack the courage for so audacious an act.

"And if it should fail, Lerk?!"

"Then I'll fix your brain with this copper rod!" the other said scornfully.

The clock on the opposite wall struck twelve. Its pendulum bob tapped lightly at the glass face of the dial below. The number 12 showed and then quickly vanished. The clock face was once again blank and white. Anyone who had not caught the number or counted the taps would not have known what time it was.

"I'll risk it! I may succeed or fail, but I'll do so greatly either way. I'm at the mercy of a woman's whims, Earth's, at that."

"Break her, and you break her whims."

"And our laws?"

"Into the canals with them!" and both friends burst out laughing.

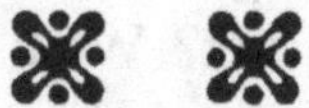

The marble tabletop was sprinkled with black liquid. Under a phosphorescent light, the atoms comprising the fluid glittered, hopping about over the table with a green glow. A young man was shining an electric bulb on the phosphorescing pinpoints of light and making careful notes on the opposite wall, covered in black canvas. The lights each surged slightly before going out, vanishing in the air. In this way, the black liquid was slowly evaporating, consuming itself and disappearing into the grooves of the marble tabletop. The electric light bulb could capture only the liquid's essence—electrical power. It now began to glow with a deep-blue light, and the researcher was satisfied. He checked off his notes on the wall and numbered them. Then illuminating them with the ray from the light bulb, he made them forever indelible.

The black surface held the chemist's secret, which only the electric light bulb could reveal.

But this current was another of his secrets. The young man stepped up to the tall window and began to smile contentedly. The substance was now ready, and it was only a matter of time until the moment was right.

The stars were sparkling in the sky. The summer night was serene, mystical. Earth shone in the vast distance, its shimmering light outshining the other stars around it. The chemist's eyes were fixed on it, and his ambition surged along with his will.

"Celestial dictation!" he cried excitedly, leaning out the window. "The fame and respect I shall win! I wonder if those ants down there can see that we're quickly catching up to them. They'll be stunned by our 'canals!' How deflated

they'll be!" And the young man burst into peals of laughter.

"Aren't you asleep yet? What are you laughing at?" came a gentle voice from below, and a pebble hit the window.

"Come up here, Iva, and you'll have a good laugh too."

Delicate footsteps pattered down the path, and a young girl ran up the stone steps. She let her long skirt fall back over her knee and knocked lightly on the door. The chemist came out to meet her and kissed her on the lips.

"You smell of phosphorus!" she said, gently pushing him away.

"You'll be smelling it often from now on, until my brain is steeped in it," he said, laughing.

"What are you going to do?" she said with a start and draped herself around his neck.

"That's my secret, darling. If I take too long to wake up, look here, you can always revive me with this electric lamp."

"My God, what are you thinking of doing? Where are you going? What if this light stops working?" She was trembling with fear and doubt.

"Then wake me with another flame, the flame of love!" he said, and he swung her to himself.

"Oh, Astor, give up this mad venture. What do you care for those foolish Earthlings? They see nothing, hear nothing, and walk with their heads bowed to the ground instead of looking to the sky," she protested indignantly.

"Darling, they call our gigantic project 'canals.' I want to let them know at last what we've created on our globe!"

"Canals? What are 'canals?'"

"I don't know either. Sometimes they say canals, sometimes they say channels."

"Meanwhile …" the girl laughed merrily.

"You be quiet, you," Astor threatened, and he kissed her laughing mouth.

"You'll tell me just what to do before you start anything, though, won't you?" she pleaded, tenderly cajoling him.

"This lamp is all there is to it!"

"Oh, God, how stubborn you are."

"Do you believe in God enough to call on him?"

"Yes, I believe in Him. The obsolete dogmas will fall, and the God of a new faith and doctrine will come."

"Oh, you puritan, you. Will you build him tabernacles too?"

"Oh, Astor, don't make fun of me but help me instead. The priests rail against us, and the scientists mock us."

"Iva, you'd better put that questionable faith aside and work with me. You're so bright, and I could use a tactful collaborator," he chided her, stroking the softly rich hair that curled loosely around her head.

"You have Lerk! I'll never enter your study as long as he's in there!" she said, angrily stamping her foot and pushing his hand away from her head.

"Why don't you like him?"

"I hate him, I hate him!" she cried passionately.

"But, Iva, my dear, control yourself!"

"He's from another land, he's a demon, and he does nothing but deceive you and lead you astray!"

"How childish and superstitious you are. I thought you were more sensible. Lerk is a hardworking, energetic man, with great will, which he uses to spur me onward in my experimentation. I'd be weak and indecisive if it weren't for him. I don't need his help, but I do need him to spur me on. I'm still lacking in courage because my love for you holds me back. But he isn't bound by any ties or scruples. He goes about his work fearlessly, uninhibited by emotion."

At these words, the young man's strong cheekbones took on a stern expression, and Iva trembled with fear and awe before him.

"He scorns and reviles our love, mocking our union. He has never loved any woman; he does not know that the beauty of life consists only in love. He's engaged to that dry old science of his and rails against us women. But he'll be sorry when he does fall in love!" She clenched her tiny fists and shook them at the window.

"So, love will turn out badly for him?" Astor laughed again, kissing the tiny, clenched fist.

"It'll overwhelm both him and his cold science!" she exclaimed angrily.

"It must be wonderful to be overwhelmed by love. I almost envy him!"

"You're an incorrigible tease," said Iva, still a little angry, and she sat down on a narrow bench. A large bird was perched on its bars, pecking at her clothes, cawing in a screeching voice.

"How are you doing, Kraa?" she asked, handing him some grain from a nearby bowl. He swallowed the seeds quickly, fluttering his wings in delight at the morsel and at her cajoling him. She took him onto her lap and stroked his ruffled feathers.

"You're looking very untidy! Clearly your master isn't looking after you. Astor, does he still drink your paints and oils?" Iva laughed merrily.

"That rascal? Yesterday he broke the mirror-tablet he was looking into."

"Apparently, he didn't like what he saw. What a sight he is!"

"Yes, and he pecked the rather fine glass into pieces and shattered it into smithereens. But I punished him by letting him go hungry, and then he went and ate the entire snack I'd prepared." Iva laughed heartily, and the bird, seeing her cheerful mood, squawked even more, as if laughing along with her.

"Look, he's laughing too!" Astor said, thrusting a slender cane toward him. With a violent leap, Kraa perched himself on the stick, and Astor went whirling around the room with him. The bird began to squawk joyfully, like a parrot, over his master's dancing.

Iva laughed like a child in the full flush of play until her luxurious hair went flying about her head. Their laughter and the mad bird's wild screeching filled the little room, echoing into the silent night.

These were the most beautiful evenings of all for the youthful Iva. She loved Astor for his lively, wholesome good cheer, for the importance of the work he did, and for his irrepressible humor as he made fun of himself for his failed experiments. He had a sarcastic way of looking at things and a wry tone, lavishing ironic comments upon himself. Then he would talk to himself in the second person in a foreign language, calling himself the worst names in his vocabulary. He was very conscientious, did not like to do anything at someone else's expense, and was not out for riches. But he was also ambitious and embarrassed about this. He would therefore keep his great ideas hidden and not confide them even to his best friends. He was friends with Lerk and worked with him but never sought him out. Lerk, however, would come to see him, much to Iva's displeasure. While Astor was handsome, wholesome, and cheerful, Lerk was unattractive and taciturn, with cryptic eyes. However, Lerk was not truly ugly. He differed from them only in being of a foreign type, and neither of them knew where he came from. They had met by chance during their studies in the city and struck up a friendship, which Lerk had nurtured with frequent visits. He had a strong will, in which Astor found support, yet out of his love for Iva, Astor himself did not care to pursue any bold ideas for inventions with him. Lerk loved explosives, and Astor feared them. Because Astor was well-to-do, he could work on his own, while Lerk worked for the government. And this made for a great difference between their situations. They often clashed in their opinions and then parted ways in anger. But Lerk would not stay angry for long and would come back because of…his love for Iva! Yet neither Astor nor Iva suspected this. Only the bird Kraa would observe the new master with round eyes and his hooked beak, pecking him fiercely on the leg when he found him nearby. Lerk would beat and scold the bird mercilessly for this.

So, love and hate went hand in hand, laying plans for their next conflict. The science of "chemistry" was to be the tool of both.

Igo Pнenomén

$\mathcal{T}$he thaw came suddenly for the snows this year, resulting in plenty of moisture to nourish the flora; and there was hope for an abundance of flowers. Iva was renowned far and wide for her green thumb. Her flowerbeds, vibrant as carpets, abounded with fragrance and color of extraordinary beauty—especially this year! For she was a florist, a virtuoso at tying and sorting bouquets. Her tall glass vases in varied hues were always filled with bouquets arranged with grace and style. Displayed on wide stone tables, they boasted a fairyland-like loveliness, and a light mist from several fountains kept them moist and fresh. Her flower nurseries, long and narrow glass structures, were constantly besieged by the buying public. The bouquets were sold in vases, each a different shape and color, with the bouquet arranged to complement it. The larger flowers with long stalks came in low-centered, bowl-shaped vases on three legs resembling pagan sacrificial goblets. Taller vases were filled with drooping, upright, and tendrilled flowers. Others still, bulbous in form, held flowers with such enormous stalks that they threatened to topple over.

Iva prevented this by tying them with ribbons to ornamental trellises placed behind. The fair gardener's taste, elegance, sensitivity, and refinement found expression with admirable grace and harmony in the glass nurseries. Iva would shake the broad fern leaves, trimming their withered fronds, and place them carefully in a vase. Her luxuriant hair was drawn back with a broad bow, and a long trailing skirt, bound with an ornamental pin, was hitched up to her side. A dainty leg peeped out from under the skirt's hem, and a long fringe of red silk, tied above the knees, dropping far down onto her calves. She wore low red shoes without heels, long ribbons fluttering about her feet at every step, tinkling with glass beads sewn onto the bows.

Iva was pretty and coquettish. Her large brown eyes were shaded by her eyelashes and by black eyebrows that slanted to one side at the same angle. This gave her face a weird expression that was always alluring and striking. Most Martians had eyebrows slanted to one side like this; but there were naturally races with different eyes, as different as your white and yellow people. Iva was of the northern race, of the Lopus nation. But her blood was mixed on her mother's side with the blood of the Uguls from the southern provinces, so she would sometimes burst out with impetuous passion. The Uguls were a cultured but warlike, proud, and imperious people, rather like your Germans.[1]

Shaking out some flowers in her outstretched arms and casting a practiced eye over a bouquet to see whether it was arranged in keeping with styles and regulations, she glimpsed an unknown man outside the window, intently watching what she was doing. She blushed as red as the fringe upon her calves and set the bouquet on the table. The stranger walked briskly into the nursery and bowed

1. *Race* (Czech *rasa*, [dated] *raça* < French *race*). In this period sense, the word could refer to a family line or pedigree but also, for example, to "Germans" or "Slavs." It indicated a group that allegedly shared certain inherited physical and mental traits. Many residents of interwar Bohemia were of combined heritage, mainly Czech, German, Jewish, and Polish.

deeply. She immediately discerned that he was a wealthy foreigner. She led him into another greenhouse to a table full of splendid flowers and vases. The foreigner gazed with surprise and interest at the proud flora from every possible land, cultivated in Iva's gardens. She accepted his silent tribute with regal pride, lifted her long skirt higher, and quickly lowered it again. The movement, coquettish and calculated, was executed with distinction, and the stranger readily paid whatever the flowers cost.

He bought all the blooms on display for a house party, to which he also invited the fair gardener. She accepted the invitation with a sweet smile, and blushing like one of the roses on her table, saw him to the door. She read his name—Igo Phenomén!—on the invitation and shuddered all of a sudden.

For some time after the foreigner's light vehicle had trundled away, Iva stood there as if stunned, clutching the white card in her fingers—*Igo Phenomén!*—Astor would speak the name with profound gravity, but she had always noticed how he shuddered at its mention. Lerk had spoken it but once and went deathly pale as he did. When she was a little girl, her mother would often warn her, "never go past the birch groves where … *Igo Phenomén* takes his stroll." She obeyed, keeping her distance from the white birch trunks glimmering in the forest's darkness. When the bells at the nearby castle rang of their own accord, the people whispered the name with a mixture of pride and awe: Phenomén.

She sat on the tabletop and contemplated the mysterious foreigner. His flowers had drooped in their vases, so she began to water them gingerly. They perked up slightly, fortified by the gentle sprinkling, but a moment later they were back to leaning over the glass rims. She sprayed them some more and opened the windows, but the flowers drooped even lower. Carefully, she inspected bouquet after bouquet for insect damage, but the stems and calyxes were spotless, with only the colors slightly faded. The tall stems in the bulbous pots were slowly breaking, as if from a violent wind, so she quickly closed the windows. The ferns that she had been so carefully tidying up a moment before had shriveled like tobacco leaves. Death swept silently over the flowers on the table's marble surface, rapped at the glass walls of the vases, and drove the life out of Flora's beautiful children. The fiery colors were fading, the scents commingling in the chaotic throes of dying.

Iva, her heart clenched in pain and her face contorted with rage, watched all her hard work wither away.

They were paid for, of course, but she would never have sold them only to meet their ruin. The blood rushed from her heart to her head in an agony of pain, the blood of the Uguls throbbing passionately to her brain, where spite and hatred for this alien foreigner boiled up. She took a large water funnel and smashed the vases, then scattered the wilting flowers. Her mouth twisted with scorn, her eyebrows standing perpendicularly as they plunged toward the middle of her forehead over the base of her nose, and a cry of immense hatred rang through the glass building: "Damn you, Igo Phenomén!"

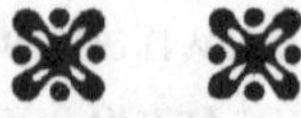

A sumptuous table had been set. Water and wine glasses stood side by side, and there were salad plates decorated with tiny flowers. Ornamentally etched forks with ivory handles lay atop the settings, their carved designs gleaming pristinely as they skewered salted slices of yellow bread.[2]

2. Yellow is the "theosophical" color for pure intellect (Carlson,

"There will be some more flowers from Iva, the gardener, and then we'll be done," said one of the girls setting the table.

"Who's going to bring them into the house? There are a hundred and fifty vases," said the valet, "and we can't carry them all."

"That's his business; it's not our job to carry vases. The flowers will wilt once they're here anyway. Everything withers under his gaze. He is the priest of a new god and has the power of the hex, so let's be on guard against him. We'd better leave the dining room before he gets here. Máv, you're so young and fair that he could easily bewitch you." Their two pairs of diligent hands flitted still more busily so as to finish quickly. They sprayed fine perfumes around the ballroom and vanished silently behind the portière. They overturned the bowls where their wages had been left, bottom upwards, and disappeared into the garden, where they took leave of each other on the path. Curious, Máv looked back at the windows one last time and drew a long breath. She would have been glad to attend so sumptuous and distinguished a banquet, but how could a poor working girl who prepared rooms for parties ever hope for anything of the kind?

As a wealthy foreign nobleman who had resided here for some time, Igo Phenomén held banquets by invitation only. He would not rank his guests according to their status and fortune, however, but according to their achievements. Máv had not yet distinguished herself in any way, nor had she been able to make her mark with her talent for arranging flowers, for some incident or other had always prevented this. The tabletop in the Phenomén household should have stood out for its style and artistry, but Máv still did not have the flowers from Iva, who was late in delivering

"Fashionable Occultism").

them. The valet would probably arrange them himself and certainly tastelessly, disrupting the entire table setting. Igo Phenomén would then sneer at the flower arranger and say she did not deserve her wages. "Ohh," Máv sighed, and she covered her face in shame and regret.

Why had Iva been late with the flowers, falling behind schedule and damaging both her own good name and Máv's reputation as an exemplary worker? Oh, God! How much suffering one person's negligence can cause, how much harm to others' reputations. Máv was ambitious, and she wanted to excel in her field at any cost. At a house like Phenomén's, she could have made her mark. But—through carelessness—the fair gardener had clipped her wings in the middle of a flight of daring and boldness. Sorrowful and angry, she rushed to Iva's gardens, but the glassed-in nurseries were locked tight, and the garden workers did not know her whereabouts.

So she returned home, vexed and out of sorts, and she flung Phenomén's princely wages into a drawer. They gave her no pleasure.

She had no idea that Iva had been wounded even more deeply, or that she had returned this prominent nobleman's money without explanation.

Astor held Iva on his lap, comforting her in every way he could.

"Don't be upset. Calm down! We'll revive those hexed flowers, and you'll set them back out in vases and send them where they belong."

"It's impossible, Astor; they're so droopy and wilted that I can't revive with any kind of water or air. But maybe that magical lamp you just built could help. If it's supposed to be able to light up your dormant brain and rouse it from slumber, perhaps it can wake the sleeping atoms of the dying flowers," Iva said sadly, laying her head on his shoulder.

Astor lifted his head sharply, his eyelids blinking firmly, and a nervous tremor ran through his limbs. An idea to the rescue! An electric current powered by the atoms of another substance could perhaps restore life to the ailing flowers. Unexpected vistas opened before his ambitious eyes, and his inventive mind eagerly anticipated a new experiment.

"Come, my darling, let's try our luck! Open the greenhouses and have new vases brought."

Iva, buoyed by his hopes, hopped down and, clasping his head, pressed a long kiss upon his eyes. "How good you are, Astor. If you succeed, my nurseries shall be saved, and the flowers won't be so quick to decay."

They crossed the large garden, where men and women were busy at work, and where water from rain and snow was collected in great marble basins. Stout women were purifying the water with filtering devices, because Iva would not allow the flowers to be sprayed with dirty water. Other women were standing over small vats of purified water and dissolving mineral salts in them. With this solution, they would cleanse any leaves that were afflicted by disease or insects. Little boys in loose shirts with rolled-up sleeves were washing the cut leaves of ferns and various palm trees for decoration. Iva employed about twenty people in the gardens, in addition to several shop girls in the nurseries.

She called one of the boys and ordered him to bring down the vases that were kept in a wooden storage shed next to the nursery. She wrote down what kind were needed and bade him to be careful not to break anything. She sent the shop girls home, drew the nearby paper window-curtains shut, hung a notice over the doorway that they were closed for the day, and carefully locked the door. The glass vases were passed through the back window by the boy, and Astor carefully arranged them on the empty table. Iva swept away the broken pieces, gathered the scattered flowers to one side of the table, and gazed sadly at the destruction.

She loved her flowers, her work, and the good livelihood that it provided. She was a merchant through and through, though her heart would sometimes ache as she sold the flowers nearest and dearest to her. It was no easy thing to part with them, but she consoled herself with a solid profit and the hope that she would grow yet more flowers.

She had an elemental logic, being neither sentimental nor given to philosophizing. She sprinkled the wilted flowers once again and sorted them carefully. Astor, having the magical lamp concealed in his cloak, had finished setting up the vases and closed the window. He directed the boy not to disturb them. He carefully covered the window with his cloak, then took out the lamp and turned it on. It lit up with violet light and cast a magical glow on the blossoms. He held it close to them, and Iva eagerly observed its effect. At first the white leaves of the caliciform flowers stood upright, and the twisted ferns straightened again, but the color of the leaves also brightened to a lighter tone.

The white elderberries, daffodils, lilies, white violets full of buds, and all the various acacias were miraculously reviving under the violet light. For some of the flowers, the lamp had to be brought closer, and some recovered when it was held at a short distance. The white camellias took on a lilac hue, and Iva cried out with joy. The roses of all colors and shades were stirring from the swoon induced by the evil eye. With trembling hands, Iva picked them up and placed them in the vases, her eyes brimming with tears of gratitude and love for the chimerical creatures that were these flowers. Astor, handsome and tall, his face beaming with pride in his work, walked round the table like a god of resurrection; and like a physician, gently and carefully, he continued to illuminate these tender, withered coronets of natural beauty.

Iva, attending him like a priestess, gathered the wounded from the sad battlefield of the marble table. Some she had broken as she beat them angrily with the funnel, and now she was ashamed of her brutality. An entire little basket was filled with completely ruined and crushed blooms. Astor illumined them once again, but they only tipped their calyxes in sorrow, since the sap of life had been severed with the stems that Iva had broken off.

A large, blood-red rose caught the violet tinge of the wondrous light that had impressed itself upon its velvety petals, and it did not fade away. Iva pressed it to her lips in pity.

"Oh, forgive me, my native beauty, I'll make it up to your progeny. They shall be queens in my gardens, and I shall name them Astor."

"You shall name them Phenomén," Astor said in a lofty voice. "If it weren't for this man, I wouldn't have managed to test out my invention. You shall send him his flowers and attend his banquet. You must wear your most flattering gown. Remember, my darling, that this lamp is our secret."

"And our fortune!" added the practical Iva, as she clung to his neck.

* Telephonic mirrors. Author's note.

Máv paced up and down the garden. All her thoughts turned toward Phenomén's house and then returned to the lovely gardener. An agonizing torment of humbled ambition drove her from place to place. She could have also made her mark today. The noble foreigner's sumptuous table was laid with the most beautiful cutlery of crystal and gold, such as her eyes had never seen. For however many tables of the nobility she had arranged, nowhere had she seen so much splendid cutlery, so many golden forks, knives, and variously shaped bowls placed on small stands beside the vases on the banqueting table.

The valet gave specific instructions on how they were to proceed but then took no further notice of them, leaving everything to Máv. She arranged everything with the pride of her noble blood, which imbued her with taste and elegance. Only the miserable flowers were still missing, those lovely blooms of Iva's that had inspired whole fairy tales. She clasped her head in her hands and could barely restrain her tears.

"Why must I grovel in humiliation when I have just as much right to sit at the nobleman's sumptuous table? He has invited all the outstanding men and women of labor, since he's holding a banquet to honor guests of talent and enterprise." Lerk, the austere researcher and friend of Astor; the great and solemn Bugev, the stargazer and scientist who was convalescing at the spa near here; the short and pugnacious Pritch, the geometer and geologist always searching and measuring, running about the fields with nervous gestures; and Mleno, the impetuous and obstinate university professor, said to have discovered a new writing system and constructed a new alphabet for an electric machine that Máv did not understand.

Women were also invited. The mighty and powerful

Lektona, who had perfected the telephone so that the apparatus displayed the speaker's image remotely. The invention had caused a sensation, eliminated the misuse of the telephone, and the glass tablets* were truly in demand. These tablets, mounted above the telephone cabinet, were animated by the faces of citizens of all states and nationalities in communication with each other.

The slender, graceful Stemfa had perfected perfume baths that women emerged from like fragrant blossoms. She had also mastered the expression of personalized scents that were imbued with the user's individual character. She had written an entire book on the subject that had sold thousands of copies.

Also invited was a messenger of the dead, the most insignificant person of all, and Máv really did not know how he had come to this honor or distinguished himself.

There came a clatter of rushed footsteps on the nearby path, and Máv, driven by an impulse, ran outside. Iva's workers were bringing large baskets of vases filled with flowers. Máv began to tremble from head to toe and immediately went to meet them. Perhaps there was something she could salvage. So agitated was she that she neither said anything nor asked any questions. She ran with tiny steps to Phenomén's house, and light-footed as a fox, she skittered through the vestibule and up the marble staircase, and she paused warily by the portière that covered the way into the banquet hall. Her keen eyes swept across the room, but she saw no one. Her joy swelled to ecstasy.

She would be alone. Oh, God, what luck!

Meanwhile the workmen had come and set up the baskets where she told them to. They knew her and obeyed her orders willingly, and then they left just as they had come, without noise or unnecessary chatter. Máv hugged the first vase with delight and kissed the bulging glass. She even kissed the flowers it held and set to work with gusto. One hundred and fifty vases, each one different, gave her plenty to do and called for the utmost artistry in the arrangements to make the table look like a garden fit for a feast. Máv succeeded. Doll-like, she whirled about in the vast banqueting hall, undisturbed by anyone and unaware that Phenomén was watching her with his evil eye. She felt safe, and so she gave free rein to her feminine caprices and coquetry. When something lay beyond her reach, she climbed upon a chair, and when even that did not help, she climbed up onto the table. First, however, she took off her tiny shoes and, dashing over the table in her stockinged feet, spun nimbly among the plates and goblets. She was scurrying like a mouse among cabbages in a field. Her heart sang with delight at what she had accomplished, proud that her ambition was fulfilled, and her artistic spirit triumphed over the finished work. She was done. The crystal glass of the vases glittered, and the flowers' beautiful scent filled the banquet hall with an intoxicating fragrance.

Máv stood in the middle of the table, her hands grasping the great chandelier, and she swung like a bird on a branch. Her nimble feet kept clear of the objects on the table, and her mouth was about to sing when suddenly the curtain parted, and there stood: Igo Phenomén! She let out a cry of horror and fell! The most imposing vase was shattered, and Máv was lying on top of it, bleeding from numerous cuts caused by the broken shards. He lifted her in his strong arms and carried her out of the banqueting hall.

The Feast of Talents

Without lovely women and beautiful flowers, the worlds would be sadder places. And so the godhead places them in every region and on every planet, kindling the lights of heaven above!

O women, you should bear this in mind and embrace virtue!

Iva put on the most beautiful gown she had in her wardrobe and shut herself up in her chamber. Not even Astor could know by what means she was enhancing her beauty. The glass baignoire in her washroom was filled with fragrant essences as prescribed in Stemfa's manual, and but a single fragrance needed to assert itself within the strongest essence for a beautiful body's individual scent to take effect. Iva was a child of nature. Always in motion among the flowers in the open air, she was suffused with the perfumes of nature to the point that she had little need of artificial fragrances. She kept them all in the washroom and followed the prescriptions for a bath. She was sensitive, and no offense was to be permitted against her delicate sense of smell. She was equally strict with her attire and knew how to dress for her stature, coloring, and style of movement. There was no fashion on the world of Mars, and women dressed according to the dictates of their taste and artistic talent. Iva's evening couture was her own creation.

A fine net fabric flowed lightly over her slender limbs and trailed behind her in a knotted train. Her bare, lovely arms were encircled in a flower trim like bracelets. Her plunging décolletage was covered by an arrangement of artificial diamonds that sparkled with every hue and cast a radiant reflection on her lovely face. Her dark, luxurious hair was swept up in a silver net and light-colored feathers that fell to her shoulders. Her peculiar eyebrows, angled to one side, enhanced her weird beauty, and her proud, arched forehead gazed haughtily in the mirror. Iva paid particular attention to her forehead. Just as your women tend and cherish the purity of the skin, so do Martian women tend their foreheads; for it was the vault and the treasury of all their thoughts. There were many who could read these arched foreheads, but one of the best decipherers of the mysterious human spirit was Igo Phenomén.

Iva gathered up all her hair from her forehead, which she now covered with the simple silver netting. Astor was already knocking impatiently on the door. He wanted to see her before she left, and he didn't want to miss this lovely sight. When she opened the door, he embraced her, rapturous and admiring.

"How lovely you are, you enchantress! Iva, keep your wits about you, be discreet, and be very careful about our… lamp. Come, I'll illumine you with it, so that no one shall outshine you." Carefully, he took from his coat the small electric lamp that he always carried with him and switched it on.

"Light up my brain!" Iva laughed merrily, "since that's what you invented it for." Astor smiled and lightly touched her forehead.

"Oh, stop!" she cried. "What is that writing I see?" And she thrust his hand away.

"What writing?" he asked, surprised.

"Leave me alone, it really is time to go." And Iva left, her brain irradiated.

She was aglow not only with Astor's light but with her love for him, her proud awareness of her own beauty and youth, and her work, for which she was paid and admired. An electric vehicle delivered her to Phenomén's house, and the valet ushered her into the vestibule. There she was introduced to the other guests, who were already gathered around the host.

The nobleman's demonic eyes ran through her like an electric current. She lowered her proud brow and made a deep bow. Phenomén gave a signal, and everyone made their way to the table. With silent commands, he had them take their places, for each chair already had the name of its guest. Iva sat on the host's right and the messenger of the dead on his left. The stark contrast between the two, so at odds in physical beauty and in their professions, was a testament to Phenomén's nature. Why had he made a point of putting these two so close together? The shrewd Iva immediately sensed the direction of his thoughts and plans, and she resolved to be cautious. She pulled her silver netting down lower over her forehead and covered her outlandish eyebrows. Phenomén caught this movement of her lovely hands, and his eyes filled with such flame that Iva quickly put her hands back on the table. A twitch ran through her slender fingers, and they inadvertently crushed the lovely rose that had been placed on her plate. Suspecting this magnificent man's dangerous game, she found herself quivering before him.

The messenger of the dead handed her a bowl of fruit and brought her thoughts into harmony and peace. The bowl circulated farther around the table, and soon an interesting conversation struck up. In a strong voice, the stout, tall Lektona explained the workings of the telephone and the operation of the magical tablet. Tonight, she was revealing the secrets of her work and the invention itself, for by law everything had to be turned over to humanity for its common use. No province was allowed exclusive ownership of any invention. Every one of them, after a certain length of time, became the property of all nations, and the governments of every country made recompense to the inventors. The spirited Martians, however, took more satisfaction in admiration and recognition than in money.

Lektona was honored tonight with a diploma and the title of scientist, presented to her by Phenomén on behalf of all governments. She would not accept the monetary reward and placed it in the bowl of the messenger of the dead. The slender and graceful Stemfa received the golden rose, a great national award, and immediately tucked it into her hair. She had the right to wear it daily as a badge of her labor and distinction. The great and solemn Bugev contented himself with a handshake from Phenomén. Others were similarly rewarded in turn, and Iva received a tightly sealed vial of unknown contents. She slipped it past the neckline of her gown and bowed deeply in gratitude. The pugnacious young Pritch then began to expound his geometrical creations with lively gestures, and he was very much annoyed that his engineers were behind in their work. He was directing the construction of the "canals," which had constantly to be repaired and rebuilt in various particulars. The quick-tempered Mleno took issue with him, and soon a quarrel broke out, a quarrel between scholars that attracted attention with its phrasing, cadences, and breadth of knowledge. The conversation sparkled with wit, tempered by erudite self-restraint, piquing the interest of the others. The feast ceased to be merely an occasion for diversion, and the banqueting hall teemed with intellectual vigor and prowess.

Iva was listening and watching it all with widened pupils and a pounding heart. She observed the figures of the men grouped in one corner of the hall and the magnificent-looking Phenomén, maintaining his composure among them. All these scientists' lofty thoughts stirred an inexpressible sense of eagerness within her.

What treasures were hidden away in these brains! Her eyes glided from one man to another, from one brow to the next, and her hands trembled with nervous agitation. She thought of Astor, his enchanted lamp, and the place that should have been his, here among these men. Yet he had not been invited!

Phenomén had ignored her flowers until now. He likely knew well enough what he had made happen, but he asked no questions about it; perhaps he thought she had replaced them with new ones. The proud blood of the Uguls rushed to her arched brow, and violently, she tore the netting from her head. Her slanting eyebrows emerged, now perpendicular to her forehead.

Phenomén withdrew from the men and approached her with a solemn step, observing her exposed, outlandish eyebrows. The two pairs of eyes met, boding ill, and the inevitable followed.

Phenomén's demonic eyes swept over the table, his gaze coming to rest on each flower. And once again, chimerical death marched silently over the gentle beauty on the table. Iva's heart cried out with pain and wounded pride. She clasped her hands behind her head and bit her white teeth into the tender lips that had uttered the cry of anger and pain.

Phenomén came and stood close before her. His handsome face, calm and impassive, inflamed others to madness. His large, deep eyes tore hearts to shreds and jolted delicate minds until they were reeling with vertigo. One could only live or die in his presence; there was no middle way. He was a man who provoked passionate love or deadly hate.

He took her hands from her head and said in a cold voice: "You have cursed me, and I shall destroy you like these flowers!"

"I shall raise them up again!" she cried at him.

"They can only be replaced!" he retorted mockingly, pressing her hands to his lips.

"They're the same ones you destroyed before!" she protested fearlessly. A sweet, strange feeling coursed through her body as he clasped her hands in his, and an odd terror filled her heart. She succumbed to his power and wrenched her hands away in desperation. The spell was broken, and a fresh wave of hatred overwhelmed her. She felt that she was as strong as he, and that a life-or-death struggle with him was impending.

"If you can resurrect them before my eyes, my love for you shall be even greater," he said boldly, bowing deeply and leaving to join another cluster of guests. She took a seat in her armchair, fixing her gaze on the wilting flowers. The guests began to take notice of this as they returned to the table.

The fair Stemfa was deeply sympathetic and expressed this to Iva with heartfelt words. She had heard the contretemps with the nobleman and thought he might have been blaming her for the delivery of old flowers cut long before. Stemfa's delicate, compassionate address had unwittingly rekindled the flame of Iva's anger and hatred.

"I shall revive them!" Iva haughtily declared, and she strode proudly out of the hall. The slender, serpentine train of her dress trailed after her up the marble staircase, and a sharp, distinctive scent emanated from her indignant blood. Phenomén caught her perfume with his dilated nostrils, and a still more passionate desire for this woman surged within him. Yet he watched calmly as she exited the hall, waiting to see how she should retaliate for the insult he had twice dealt her.

Iva returned a half-hour later. Reassured by Astor's kisses, she pressed the enchanted lamp to her bosom and walked proudly across the hall. This nobleman, who had twice ruined her work, would have to make restitution to her yet again. Now he must shower Astor with respect and distinction, for Astor was certainly the equal of these men. Iva wanted him at her side as a man of renown, in this hall and attending the feast of talents where every ambitious heart longed to be invited.

Phenomén represented all the states that honored these heroes of the intellect. "I want him proud and victorious at my side, my darling boy," thought Iva, and she stepped up to the table. Lerk blocked her way. He had followed the scene with the nobleman, jealousy in his eyes, watching her exit, and anxious to know whether she would return. He asked where she had been and what had happened. She dismissed him with a careless toss of her head and took her place proudly by the flowers.

With a modest movement, she unfastened her outfit and pulled the lamp from her bosom. Then, proudly, oblivious to all, she walked round the table and touched the violet light to the flowers' withered coronets. They remained bent over, insensate to the magical light that the fair gardener bore them. Everyone gathered around her, their eyes watching her actions with astonishment. Lerk was close at her side and Igo Phenomén behind her, so that she could feel his breath on her bare neck. Stemfa installed herself in a nearby armchair, and the other scientists, nodding their heads, positioned themselves so they would miss none of this peculiar scene.

Iva was trembling from head to toe. Under the influence of so many gazes and her stormy pride, she felt she must emerge victorious or go down in moral defeat in her attempt. Her proud courage began to wane as the light of the electric bulb faded. Every cell of her blood was pouring swiftly, invisibly, into that light, dimming its glow. The white-hot filaments were going out like charred threads, the purple glass returning to its original white color, and the magic of the wondrous fire fading like the scent of the wilting flowers on the table. The small lamp dropped onto the table and Iva into the nearest armchair.

White hands covered her face, now drained, and her head drooped to her breast. The silver net in her hair had shifted down to her forehead, and Iva remained profoundly silent. Only occasionally did a low, gentle whisper filter into her ears, but no one dared disturb her with prying questions or inappropriate remarks. All sensed that a great struggle, mute and invisible, had been waged. Two strong wills had clashed and struck at each other with a bellicose sword; hatred had collided with love; and the eternal laws of man with the laws of woman.

Lerk retrieved the fateful lamp and examined it carefully. He found nothing unusual about it; it was like any other. Only the wires were interwoven differently, forming the two figures of a double zero.[1] He lay it back on the

---

1. Zero symbolizes the infinite in theosophical numerology (Blavatsky, "Stars and Numbers"). Translator's note.

table and slipped out of the hall, where there was nothing more for him to do. In Phenomén's household, the utmost decorum was the rule. And his decorum dictated that he warn Astor to fetch his prostrate mistress.

Within minutes, he was in Astor's laboratory, and in a few brief words he told of what had happened.

"She has plunged into a profound silence, and you'd best quietly fetch her."

"What about my lamp?"—Astor asked, greatly concerned.

"It's gone out, and the bulb looks no different than a normal white one," Lerk said curtly. "You should be the one to handle that invention and not entrust it to a woman! There are laws of nature that men can master better than women. Come and retrieve your discarded invention. You can either captivate them with your brilliant idea or quietly fetch the lamp. Nobody knows what's inside it—only Igo Phenomén!"

"That great mind has already extinguished the lives of the poor flowers once, and now he's extinguished them a second time. But why did he do it? Why does he insult Iva in front of his guests, the scientists? What has she done to him?" asked Astor, the whole of his frank and open nature in revolt against the nobleman.

A jealous expression distorted Lerk's face. He had intuited Phenomén's love for the fair gardener and wished him to be even more defeated and hated by Iva. Astor must stir up this hatred with his own spurned love.

And to that end, Lerk was inciting him against Phenomén. Astor quickly put on his formal clothes. Under the influence of Lerk's provocation, however, he stripped off these clothes and put on his ordinary work overalls. He wanted to offend against the etiquette in Phenomén's household and to disrupt the social decorum.

Lerk was already rubbing his hands with glee that he could kill two birds with one stone: he could make Astor a social pariah and humiliate Iva. It would then be difficult for Astor's invention, if in fact there was anything to it, to succeed, and the ambitious Iva would fall into his own arms. Lerk was preparing a spectacular invention of his own, and that might help him to win this proud girl's heart after all.

They hurriedly followed the roads and footpaths that led to the nobleman's house and went directly into the great room where all the guests had assembled. His face a mask of excitement, Astor made fleeting bows to those nearest him before rushing straight into the banqueting hall, where Iva was still sitting in profound silence, Stemfa beside her. Astor touched her bent neck with a kiss, Iva threw back her head violently and hurled herself out of her seat, which toppled over with a loud crash. She took her place at his side, pointing in silence to the wilted flowers and the extinguished lamp.

Captivated by the extraordinary event unfolding before their eyes, the scientists reconvened in the banqueting hall. The gigantic struggle between the two minds had been a spectacular one, and only Martians could appreciate its power. With a low murmur, they assumed their places around the table once more. They took no offense at Astor's work overalls and followed his sensitive hands with the eagerness of scientists. Using the magic in his nerves, he lit the lamp, and he gazed at Iva with eyes full of love.

Standing grave and silent before him, her face was aglow with love and pride in the beloved man who had come in victory to deliver her from humiliation and to lay his own claim to fame.

She sensed a new current flowing in her veins, one that lacked the urgency of offended pride. It was a pride filled with quiet joy, the exquisite triumph of toil and effort. This pride was justified and belonged to them both, for the world of the Martians exalted it above all glory and profit.

By the power of mental suggestion, Astor yielded to this stream of emotion, and he solemnly raised the shining lamp in the air. Large and handsome, his face illuminated by love for both a woman and the dying blossoms, he strode from one vase to another and, like a god of light, infused the enchanted electric current's power into the dejected stalks of the lovely flowers—which, rallied by the magical power of love surging from this fine-looking man's heart, rose on their stems and puffed out their calyces until their undeveloped buds burst forth.

The foliage of the southern sun was again ablaze in all its glory!

Astor's miraculous deed complete, he put away the lamp, kissed Iva on her proud forehead and offered her his arm. He bowed silently on all sides and walked out of the great room with an easy step. Iva pressed her lips between her teeth, stifling a passionate sob of love and pride at his victory.

As frenzied cheers and applause shook the banqueting hall, Astor's name flew from everyone's lips. Lektona rushed to the nearest telephone, and soon the wires were singing his glorious praises to all the states and provinces.

Thus do Martians celebrate their inventors: not with wreaths of laurel but with the victorious procession of an immortal name!

The Dignity of Labor

The huge structures of the bridges were creaking under the torrent of runoff from the mountain ridges. This year's snowpack had melted rapidly, and the parched ground could not absorb the excess moisture. Water shot through the underground pipeways, bursting to the surface and spraying high like fountains. The cheers and shouts of the boaters riding the streams of water rang far and wide. Men, women, and children were casting nets and catching fish, scouting out the roots of various fragrant herbs torn from somewhere in the mountains and borne by the torrent to lower-lying regions. Engineers and surveyors were making their way over the floodlands with studious care and inspecting the bridges as they were cleared by trains at breakneck speed. The supporting arches, poised over the planet's surface and spread wide like huge nets, trembled at their foundations with the rumbling of the trains. In these arches, the gigantic work of the Martians encapsulated every thought that had coursed through the brain of any inventor or worker.

These arches concealed the cables and magnetic wires for every medium of communication, so the powerful atmospheric electricity never sent messages astray.

Electric current propelled the trains forward, and the lights of every grid and network illuminated the entire landscape. The power of the planet's magnetic core was so well harnessed that it even coursed across the bold sweep of the bridges' arches.

The geometer Pritch always laughed that the Martians could even stop the planet's rotation about its axis. Iron, the magnet, and the Martian were the three driving forces of a globe whose population was of the highest intelligence and most liberal opinions but also the most proudly demanding.

Martians are ambitious, madly so, and this ambition drives them onward to the most impossible inventions and to breakneck progress.

In the planet's solar orbit, twenty-three of your months in duration, every individual's appetite and capacity for labor thrive, and each makes his way through life to the enthusiastic cheering of all others who labor.

No Martians have ever been idle!

Their cultures have evolved in iron and the magnetic core as their history has blazed its trail with sword and blood. The banner raised high by the "strong individuals" has always had the same motto in every century: "Work and Its Recognition."

The Martians are proud workers! So proud that they die a voluntary death when they can no longer labor since their faith does not deter them from suicide.

They have come to see the indefatigable worker as their savior. He did not come to them in the form of Christ. The world of Mars has a different composition, and the Christian faith could therefore find no place there. This planet requires energy and a constant struggle unleashed against the elements of nature. Christ's tender mercies would stifle this energy. *Their savior was the proud god of labor and innovation.* But this god has also taught a great love for one's fellow man, and so Martians are compassionate and courteous to the utmost degree, thoughtful and considerate. *The laws of labor are at the foundation of the curriculum, and entire generations are educated on that basis.* He who does not work is a miscreant and a traitor to his homeland to be forcibly enlisted in the ranks of public laborers. Teachers, by their classroom lectures, awaken young hearts to the pride of labor, and the public must perforce also value, compensate, and admire labor. In this way, ambition, the love of labor, and the planet's welfare are fostered. Magnificent new cultures blossom overnight, like pond lilies on the surface of the waters, and every moment finds a spectacular invention taking some state or nation by surprise.

Thanks to this world's general prosperity, the spirit is set free, its wings not beaten down by poverty or want as it flourishes boldly.

In the desire for work, prejudices and titular privilege have been swept away, and the legal codes have transformed. *Women are placed on an equal footing with men,* and love freely chosen between two people is sacred and inviolable. Marriage has been toppled; because of pride in labor, there is no place for prostitution. Children take their mothers' names, not their fathers'. Hers is the child, it was conceived within her, born of her, and so it takes her name. It is therefore hers and not the man's. Thus have the shame of extramarital relations and the shunning of the illegitimate child been done away with. When a woman, according to your notion, is "taken as a wife," she keeps her own name, and is always her own person and not the man's.

She is as free as a man, works like a man, and therefore has no need for someone else's name. Her individuality is proud and self-sufficient, and she takes up with a man only out of love. If she feels no such love, she remains single, proud in her work and her independence. But in Martian conditions, there is a loving man for every woman, because *there are no more murderous wars,* and because more men than women are born there.

Instead, two or three men will vie for the love of one woman. A woman's character deepens in consequence of this, her love strengthens, and she is drawn to only one man, to whom she can never be unfaithful. But if there should be a separation, that is her affair, a purely personal one, and no authority or prejudice may interfere.

Martians are proud, unassailable. They jealously guard their families and devise all sorts of pleasures for them to enjoy. They are passionate and chivalrous in love. Their spiritual life is highly developed yet does not extend to mysticism. *The Martians are practical and do not go in for writing poems; nor are they musically inclined.* The Martian works, builds, and loves! The small globe on which he lives is a veritable trusswork of bridges and arches, because anything on its surface would be washed away by the water. *The enormous rivers covering the entire land roar in the concrete streambeds that link them to prevent their flooding the entire planet. Hence your name for them: "canals" or "channels."* There are so many of them, of these rivers and streams outside the natural waterways, that the Martian can build no surface railways and must raise everything into the air. *The globe of Mars is encompassed by these bridges and railways.* Yet this regulation of the rivers has required superhuman strength, just as the railways have in turn required superhuman innovations. Thousands of generations have labored on these intricate works, and that is why the Martian feels offended when he hears you call them "canals" or "channels." For this appellation means something quite different to him.

Owing to their world's abundant irrigation, the Martians have two to three harvests a year. The harvest is rich and bountiful. Oh, my child, the Martian is proud, rich, and blessed, and for all this—he has only his labor to thank. Though his world be six times smaller than yours, it is a model of order and prosperity.

The cemeteries on Mars are splendid parks. The bodies are not buried in graves, because the water would inundate them, but set on high columns in artistically rendered sarcophagi, wherein the coffin rests with the embalmed body of the deceased. The top of the coffin is covered with a lid of marble or metal wrought by artisans. Side by side they stand in continuous rows, with broad paths running in between. Tall palm trees sway over the sarcophagi, and climbing plants wind about the slender columns. Golden letterboxes are suspended from the lampposts, and the messengers of the dead fill them with letters of congratulations or posthumous testimonials sent by the bereaved. *The people take reverence for the dead deeply to heart,* for everyone is convinced that the dead read these letters. No dead person is forever erased from the rolls of the living; the family keeps up a "correspondence" with him that the post office handles. After a year, the letters are collected from the boxes and burned at the feasts of the dead. The dead do not wish to be excluded from the work and concerns of the living, and the bereaved therefore never inflict this grief upon them. Otherwise, by the tender bonds of posthumous communications, they readily show themselves to the living, because they are neither dreaded nor treated as if they were dead.

In the Martian faith, the dead are not released into purgatories or into the wayward paths of an unknown astral realm as are yours. You have misunderstood Christ's doctrine, and a Martian would never accept it in this way, for he continues to work and create even after death, whereas your dead wander in Purgatory. Your Christian faith still bears the traces of pagan error, and the Martian therefore scoffs at you and has no understanding for you. Both your cultures and your beliefs are repugnant to him, and he detests idle humanity. But he watches your planet by means of marvelous inventions and magnificent telescopes. He irradiates his deep nights with piercing, dazzling spotlights, and he shines massive electric lights over his cities and villages.

I love this world passionately, and I would never return to yours!

Your Earth's perpetual darkness would torment me, with its gloomy streets and houses, and the uninspired construction of its towns and villages.

So I understand and sympathize with you, for you are lonely in the darkness, pining away without sunshine or love.

O world of Mars—world of light and love—hail to thee!

MOONSTRUCK

On the thick carpets in Phenomén's bedchamber stood Máv, her hair down, her eyes feverish. She would stand that way for hours every day, her thin arms dangling limply at her sides.

Her long white robe rippled toward the ground, covering her small feet in their green slippers. She was standing like a white flower on a green leaf, listening. Her agitated nerves were on the alert, waiting for any sound in the corridor, any click of the door.

Her nerves were fraught. After her ill-fated fall on the banqueting table, she suffered a concussion, and once her health had improved slightly … a shock to her heart. She loved Phenomén. The handsome, manly aristocrat himself, proud and powerful, had applied cold compresses to her fevered head and straightened the perspiration-soaked hair above her brow with a gentle hand. She opened her eyes timidly, like a young bird in its nest, and quickly closed them again. When she recovered, he paid her double wages and sent her home.

Yet Máv came back, wearing a long white robe and green slippers. She came in stealth, her eyes closed and lips painfully clenched. A moon was then out, aglow in rosy tints, a few small clouds clustered round it like a guard of honor. It peered into all the windows and saw Phenomén standing at one of them, looking out into the night. Within his handsome head, a stubborn will was vying with a defiant love, and a burning desire for the lovely gardener tormented his heart. Solitary and unobserved, in an unguarded moment, he parted his arms at the open window—and caught the tiny Máv.

She had come like a ray of light cast by this moon, gingerly traversing the eaves of the roof, clambering past the ledges, and slipping down to him through the window with a supple movement. He embraced her in dismay and had her stand in the middle of the room. Her eyes were closed tight, her tiny body trembling with cold. In her hair, a bouquet of snowflake flowers was fixed with a green ribbon. She had come like a dead woman from the grave who has left her wreaths behind.

"Máv!" he whispered, his breath light upon her face. She opened her eyes and gazed into his. She did not know where she was; she thought he had appeared to her in a dream, and that he would quickly vanish away again. She ran her hand through her hair and pulled out the bouquet of snowflakes. With that, she was now fully awake.

A thousand vague feelings and conjectures were whirling through her mind. How did she get here?

She remembered how she had lain down after a warm bath once she had combed her hair, pulled it back in a green ribbon, and tucked the bouquet of snowflakes inside.

They were flowers that Phenomén loved. In her loneliness, she had looked forward to dreaming of him if she went to sleep with his flowers. Yet now she was seeing him not in a dream but standing before her in the flesh, and she was in a nightgown no one had ever seen her in. A deep flush suffused her cheeks, and tears of shame filled her eyes. He wrapped his arms around her and held her to his chest. The splendor of the night had brought him this child full of shyness and love.

It was now a second accident that laid her in his arms again. He answered to no one, and Máv did not belong to anyone either. He laid her down on his bed and removed her green slippers. Closing the window, he drew the curtain, and smiled. Men of his sort always have a strange smile.

Such beautifully chiseled lips inspire your trust, but the tightened corners thrill you.

It is the smile of a demon, a smile that draws you in and takes you captive.

Máv was trembling on the bed in fear of love and of him. She did not want to be his, nor did she want to lose him again. She could have left, but she lacked the will. And even if he did let her go, she would remember him again with a fierce longing that would carry her back over the rooftops and over the balconies to his window. He approached her and kissed her on the lips.

"Máv, you may leave, of course, if you wish! Jeroma shall dress you, and the valet shall see you home. You don't have far to go," he said, his voice solemn, but his eyes held her in place.

At the sound of his firm voice, she rose to her feet, put on her slippers, and walked backwards toward the door. Straining her will to the utmost, she then violently tore herself from his hypnotic gaze and took hold of the door handle. Down slid her slender hand, and slowly it sank toward the ground as if broken at the elbow, catching at the drapery in the doorway. His strong will was holding her erect, but when it turned away, she would droop without his handsome eyes upon her.

He enfolded her in his arms and carried her back to the bed. He also did as his honor bade him, and he gave her medicine that would stimulate her resistance against himself. She took a few drops and laid her head on the white pillows. Great tears rolled down her cheeks, the tears of a mute love that demanded nothing, asked nothing, and promised nothing.

She was young, pure, and resigned to submission; it was all the same whether the winds tore her to pieces or the sun warmed her, whether she grew into a beautiful woman or perished in the frost of his breath. She was like the lovely Iva's flowers, magnificent in their blooming but mortal before his will and under his gaze.

"Máv," he said, bending again over her face, "you may return home if you want."

She did not know what wanting was. She wanted to work like any other woman; she was full of illusions about life, and she wanted to achieve excellence, living in independence, public recognition, and admiration. She longed for distinction at the hands of Phenomén, who would speak and praise the workers of every state and nation.

He was the Minister of Worldwide Labor and Progress. No wonder she had succumbed to the ambition inherent in everyone, especially when she had the opportunity to decorate his table. An accidental fall, however, had struck her down in her labor's joyous flight and paralyzed her ambition. Love then saw to the rest. Now here she was, lying on his bed, hot kisses on her lips. Her nerves were trembling like hoarfrost in a chilling wind. She knew that in his arms, she might live or die.

She could feel the overwhelming power of his personality and moaned softly.

Her eyes locked again, her arms rested on the white pillows, and her tiny feet slid off the now-warm bed. Reluctantly, he put her green slippers on her feet and opened the window with a rapid movement; like a soul from the grave, Máv floated silently through the window, crossed the balcony with light steps, clambered over the ledges, and in a moment her slender, petite figure was striding across the rooftops without a single false step. She left as pure as she had come, for she had warmed the bed of the powerful nobleman for only a brief moment. The pale blossoms of the snowflakes lay on the floor, and Igo Phenomén kissed them reverently.

The fair sleepwalker could not leave through the door of her own will, so it was another will that took her off through the window.

Igo Phenomén would wait for the fair maiden at the open window every day thereafter.

Lerk was sitting on the roof of his house. He was scanning the heavens with a marvelous telescope, searching for a fixed point. The night was as clear and translucent as the water of a lake. The lovely star of Earth was twinkling in the depths of space, flirting with his perfect instrument. He was its owner, proud and possessive. No other eye had peered down the long tube but his own. He made his discoveries in the heavenly canopy alone, and he kept his notes and maps carefully hidden. Although a chemist, he also took an interest in stargazing. Educated, serious, and taciturn, he had a passionate heart that sought vengeance when wronged.

He sat brooding in a deep armchair. His mind was exhausted by his forlorn love for Iva, and he could think only of how to tear her away from Astor and bind her to his own passionate heart. But the proud and boastful woman of labor was devoted to her love, despite the powerful Phenomén's ardor and Lerk's vengeful heart. He knew the handsome nobleman's pride, and a contest was brewing between the two men.

Martians find it a pleasure to vie for love, and the most marvelous of inventions have resulted from this contest over a woman, when a man's ambition was provoked to a frenzied pitch and his mind would spill over with brilliant ideas. Just as your poets become immortal in their praise of love for a woman, so does the pragmatic Martian reach his peak in the contest for love. The victor consecrates his invention in her name, and the defeated toils feverishly onward to forget.

And thus does the goddess of labor triumph over all hearts. The world of Mars is beautiful, alight with love, ambition, and the pride of labor.

Nearby, the proud arches of the bridges that float over the broad river were brightly lit with electric lights. The fixtures were glowing in every color, casting their tinted lights deep into the water. Large timber boats were plying the river and the boatmen singing wistful songs of distant homes. Trains were rumbling over the bridge and sirens whistling to warn planes to avoid the slender telegraph poles, their lightning rods' golden spikes glittering in the sea of electric lights. Occasionally there was a hiss from a flying mail coach like a cylinder in a huge wire net, suspended from the side of the bridge. Every inch of the bridge was put to use. The watchhouses would exchange cautionary messages using electric signals by day and in the evening, warning lights.

Like a long journey into eternity, these bridges were full of bustle, hum, and life as the towns and villages lay slumbering down below, scarcely disturbed by the quiet running of the electric autos and light vehicles. Floodlight stations on the mountains and hills lit the riverbanks with magnesium lamplight.

The Martian breathed an electric air, so to speak, making

the most of this power flowing through space. With it, he propelled planes and vehicles, trains and ships, powered every incandescent bulb and lamp, and tempered the lightning of the storms that frequently jolted the suspension bridges with fury, threatening to cast them down from their proud heights. A globe full of iron and magnet supplied them with an endless quantity of these electric currents; even the typewriters wrote with this energy, and every human limb was saturated with it.

Within this energy's rhythm and tempo, life eddied the same way in every nation on Mars. This power had likewise become a compelling force for peace throughout the entire world and made wars quite impossible. Inventions of this or that sort and technique were in the possession of every state, and for a neighbor to invade another with a unique weapon was an impossibility. Disciplined, culture spread civilization's wings over the entire world, for all nations were equal. *Freedom* was the sole banner of every province. While this freedom was also bloodied by millennia of evolution that had been forded in streams of blood, *every planet in the Universe was nevertheless redeeming its crown of martyrdom, as was every individual being*. A different Savior came to each world, showing the way toward the one God of the Universe. The divine promises were written in every temple on stone tablets, *and a single law, never to be transgressed, reigned in all the worlds: "Thou shalt love thy neighbor!"*

Lerk swiveled his telescope around and pointed it not at the sky but at the far side of the bridge. The tiny figure of a girl was walking along the taut telephone wires like an acrobat on a tightrope. Her green slippers barely touched the swaying lines, so lightly did she carry herself, her arms crossed over her breasts. The young man watched her in horror, afraid lest she fall and shatter on the wide embankment's stone pavement. The telephone wires ran past his rooftop, and he waited eagerly to see whether she would reach him. Her approach was rapid enough that he could hear the singing that accompanied her ærial journey. He suddenly caught the tune and the words, and tears came to his eyes. He knew these songs, which were foreign to the local population. They were the songs of Homay, songs of the distant mountains that embraced his native fields. He was a stranger in this land. Who then was this girl who knew the tales of his homeland? Sweet memories of the beloved faces of his parents and his siblings filled his heart with peace.

His passionate desire for a woman was giving way to another emotion that this girl evoked within him. Longing to embrace this dear vision of distant mountains, he opened his arms and caught the tiny Máv. Gently and carefully, he set her in the armchair and gazed into her sleeping face. Her little mouth was blue with cold, since she had been wandering for hours in the cold expanses of space.

He took her in his arms like a small child and carried her to his room, where he laid her on the sofa and covered her with a broad shawl. She let him do as he wished without waking up. She was no longer singing and was in a deep sleep. He looked at her and tried to remember whether he had seen her somewhere before.

She was a complete stranger to him. Absorbed in his studies and lovesick for Iva, he took no notice of any women, and especially not of such tiny ones as Máv. He was most attracted to a woman who was tall, lovely, and proud like Iva. This kept him continually engaged in the contest; his spirit would never have loved a woman who succumbed to him easily. He wanted to struggle for her, to wrest her from someone else, and that was why he looked down on Astor and Phenomén. He was even willing to use wicked means if only a good outcome could be achieved.

Máv stirred and opened her eyes. She distracted him from his deep thoughts with a soft and timorous question:

"Aren't you afraid of Phenomén?" He looked at her in surprise and said defiantly:

"No, I'm not! Why do you ask, who are you, and what is your name?"

"I am Máv, an arranger of banqueting halls. For the second time today, I'm now lying in a stranger's bed. I don't know what's happening to me, I'm not well, and I have no will."

"Where were you the other time?" he asked, a feeling of revulsion rising within him. With her confession, the beautiful poetry of his native mountains that she had brought with her quickly evaporated. Was she a loose and wicked girl?

"On the bed in Igo Phenomén's room," Máv said calmly. The hidden evil of wickedness and vengefulness echoed within him once again. He thought gleefully that he could use this affair as a weapon against the nobleman. A proud and respected man would content himself with an insignificant girl such as Máv only to satisfy his own base lusts. Lerk relished the blow he would deliver to Phenomén should the nobleman make a serious play for Iva.

"Igo Phenomén let me leave pure and inviolate. I hope, sir, that you will do the same," said Máv, and she crossed her arms against him.

"How did you get in to see him? Were you not invited?"

"I don't know."

"You're not well, and surely you live alone, with no one to look after you at night. Stay with me, Máv. I'm also alone, and I'm a foreigner here. You know the beautiful songs of Homay, and you'll sing them for me."

"My mother was a Homay and taught me these songs. My father built a great telegraph station in the Homay mountains, and he met my mother there."

"What nationality was your father?"

"A Peruk from the town of Salova."

"I'm also a Peruk," Lerk cried joyously.

"You shouldn't shout such things aloud, sir, unless you want to be hated in this region. Peruks are still secretly hated here."

He was taken aback and quickly shut the door. "Tell me, Máv, won't you stay with me until you're well? You can't stay alone like this. Do you know how you got here?"

"It was desire that bore me to him, and the songs of Homay to you," Máv said dreamily.

So, she did not know how dangerous her journeys were. He felt compassion for her and again invited her to stay. In childlike simplicity, she threw her arms around his neck and promised she would. She trusted him because she did not stir his passion, besides which, they were drawn together by memories of their native land, and Máv was suffering from great loneliness. She felt at ease in his cozy room; he did not order her around in a stern voice, hold her down with his eyes, or paralyze her with his will. On the contrary, Lerk was making polite requests of her, and so he came up against the sharp spike of her will.

"How old are you, Máv?" he asked, stroking her small hands.

"I am seven years old."*

"So young and already all alone? Now sleep, little one, I'll make you a warm drink." He kissed her tenderly,

* A Martian year has 23 months. Author's note.

covered her up carefully, and went to the other room to make the drink.

Yet he had forgotten to close the window that led to the rooftop; and so it came to pass that before he brought the drink, Máv had left again just as she had come, pure and warmed by the stranger's bed. Lerk saw that she was already upon the telephone wires, and he flung away the little cup with the drink. He trained his telescope on the tiny figure, dropped to his knees … and burst out in tears. This proud worker, unapproachable and aloof, wept as memories of a lost homeland, briefly revived by this unfortunate and tender creature, flooded back to him.

Celestial Dictation

"**Y**ou're a famous man now. At the next feast of talents, you'll be sitting with the other scientists and inventors. I wonder what honors are in store for you."

"None!" Astor exclaimed, bursting into hearty laughter.

"Why none?" Iva wondered, looking at him angrily. "The entire room was watching and admiring your invention."

"What a child you are, darling, and how rampant is your pride! What honors could there possibly be for me, and from whom? I'll never hand my invention over to the world, since it wouldn't do anyone any good," laughed Astor, in fine humor as he always was when quarreling.

"Why shouldn't you? Why wouldn't it do anyone any good?" Iva cried indignantly, tugging at the fringe of her tunic. "You have no ambition. You're not a real man," and she stamped her foot angrily.

"Why would people have anything to do with my lamp? They'd take it up and down the gardens and nursery greenhouses trying to bring dying flowers back to life. That wouldn't give you anything to be happy about. Because then you wouldn't be able to sell a single vase, darling, since everyone would have enough flowers, and the kind that would never perish. And when they did start to wilt, people would simply illumine them with my lamp, and the flowers would come back to life again," Astor laughed, and he kissed her on the lips. She stared at him in astonishment and said nothing, for she understood that he was right. She was too practical a businesswoman to want to shutter the nurseries that brought her a living and the joy of both labor and life.

"I don't know what you even invented it for, then," she said disappointedly.

"For myself. The lamp enlightens me for celestial dictation!" he said evenly, with a kindly smile.

"*Ce-les-tial dic-ta-tion!*" she repeated after him, and she threw her arms in the air. "What is *that?*"

"My secret, darling!"

"Oh, get on with you! You're all secrets. I don't like them; I want to know everything. Tell me openly and straight out. What are you going to do with that lamp if you won't let it be put to use?" she started to fume again.

"I've already told you. You'll use it to wake my dormant brain if I've been asleep too long under hypnosis. But it must only be done with great love. If pride guides your hand, then I shall never wake again and shall remain on Earth."

"Is that where you're going? What is there for you to do there? All the scientists and stargazers find Earth alarming. Why should you care about *it* so much when there are millions of others like it in the universe? Your books and writings teach that the women there are immoral, and the men wade in blood," said Iva, angrily flinging aside the spray of flowers she had just finished making. She felt no regret at breaking the fragile petals that were glued to the spray's framework.

"Oh, darling, we're getting closer and closer. In a matter

of years, we'll be so close to them that we can almost look in their windows. Our stargazers have perfected maps, our opticians telescopes, our engineers instruments to intercept signals, and our technicians light emitters to hail them with. Our chemists are already working on sensitive compounds to make the penetration of Earth's heavy atmosphere possible," Astor spoke enthusiastically.

"What about you?" she interjected impatiently.

"What about me?"—Astor placed both hands on his broad chest and lifted his eyes heavenwards.

"I'll be there well ahead of them—through celestial dictation!"

Iva made an angry curtsy and left the room. Astor was still gazing at the heavens, oblivious to her angry departure.

The dark chamber was illuminated by a single lamp that Astor had covered with a gauze cloth. He put the narrow divan against one wall so that its open side was facing the window. He drew a heavy curtain of a deep crimson hue over the little window, placed a wide bowl on a low pedestal, filled it with water, and dropped a handful of some kind of mineral salts into it. The salt began to effervesce, creating a dirty foam on the water's surface. He collected some in a silver spoon that he held over a flame to reduce. Then he pounded the salt into a fine powder and sealed it tightly in a small container that he plunged into the water in the bowl. It could be kept there safely. He placed a strange apparatus of odd dimensions and shapes at the head of the bed.

Having prepared everything in this way, he fasted for several days and bathed daily. He had no contact with Iva, since she was angry with him and would not come to see him. Over that time, he grew somber and would not let even Lerk come near him. No one knew about his dark little chamber or what he was doing there. He wrote a long, serious letter to Iva telling her what to do should he not wake up in seven days at one in the morning. He also wrote a last will and enclosed it along with the letter. On the final day before the experiment, he bathed thrice, drank a hot decoction of some spices, closed the door, and lay down on the divan. He immersed himself in fervent prayer, connecting with the Spirits of Space and summoning them to his aid. Like molten gold, the strange device at his head would glow as he prayed. Then it slowly dimmed as Astor's thoughts grew feebler, and it went out altogether as the chemist fell unconscious.

A thin stylus was clicking against the dark disc rotating below it, all under a glass cover hidden in the bowels of the machine. It was like your gramophone records, turning round and round. The needle was poking dots and dashes into it and quivering like the magnetic pointer in a compass. Occasionally a violet or blue light would flash on the disc, and the sensitive instrument would give a slight shudder.

For the rest, there was dead silence in the little chamber. Astor was in a deep hypnotic trance, the tones of his young, manly face darkening, his eye sockets deepening, his cheekbones standing out more clearly, and his nose protruding more sharply. His broad chest faltering as he breathed, his arteries stilled, and his entire organism grew weaker as a mask of death settled upon him.

Iva was walking in the garden with the trail of her dress proudly raised, slung over her left elbow. Her weird eyebrows were almost fixed perpendicular to her forehead in anger at Astor. He had led her out of that hall proudly, triumphantly, and to frenetic applause, and now he would take nothing seriously. Any other man would have eagerly seized upon that rare opportunity and claimed his due. Surely *Lerk* would have taken full advantage of this; he was fired with ambition that knew no bounds. For the first time, Iva began to compare the two young men to each other. Lerk may not have been as handsome or good-natured as Astor, but his name had more of a cachet to it. He was a frequent guest at Igo Phenomén's, and that itself counted for something. He worked in secret for every country, and no one even knew what nationality he was. Proud and aloof, he made an impression. Iva did not like people whom she could read like a book, because she hated what was commonplace. Proud and defiant herself, she had many secrets that she would not confide even to Astor. She was an individual through and through, self-possessed, and would have renounced even love were it not for the injury this would do to her pride.

And so, Astor's heart was in danger from this selfish pride as he lay asleep in the dark little chamber. This striking beauty wanted to make her mark at his side in Phenomén's home, but still Astor slept on, while her offended pride and disappointed ambition kept hounding her from place to place.

It was springtime. The beautiful acacia blossoms were hanging from the trees like grapes, full of honey and a charming fragrance. The lovely avenues of these trees were especially well-tended in Iva's orchards. Their blooms enhanced the artistry of her slender vases. Igo Phenomén was a great admirer of these flowers, and he would buy them by the vaseful day after day. He paid in pure gold, courtly smiles, and smoldering looks. Iva, in her pride and desolation, even began to flirt with him and no longer shrank from his hands as he pressed hers to his lips and covered them in hot kisses. Her head was swimming in a too-sudden and unexpected intoxication—in which the vanished Astor was forgotten.

She attended several parties at the great nobleman's house as Lerk escorted her there in his vehicle. This astute man was wary of asking after her friend. He had seen the rift between the two lovers and wanted to exploit it to his own advantage. With one phrase after another, he would hold Astor up to scrutiny, casting him in an unfavorable light in both Iva's and the great nobleman's eyes. The disgruntled Iva would listen with gratification, for Astor had been away from home for six days, and he had not thought to write her a single line. Day after day had gone by like this, her anger unabated.

She had not even inquired at Astor's house, avoiding the risk of running into his servant. Although his house adjoined her garden, Iva never looked in at his windows, their curtains drawn as if to show that he had left without even saying goodbye. Tears of anger came to her eyes, but she proudly wiped them away, not wanting to remember him.

Lerk called on her every evening and regaled her with fiery descriptions of his inventions, of the international admiration and recognition he had won in the form of various honors, diplomas, and numerous awards. Fame and fortune awaited him, and he wanted to lay it all in this beautiful woman's lap for a single smile of love. Iva would turn her lovely head and listen like a queen for whom all these wonders had been prepared. In her desolation, her anger, and her rupture with the man she loved, her ambition had been whipped into a frenzy. Lerk was charging down upon this heart with all the defiant strength of the Peruk race and attempting to sweep up its owner in his passionate arms. She knew she could have either of these two men for the asking, either Lerk or Phenomén. Her feminine diplomacy was lying in wait and biding its time. The handsome nobleman was nothing like Lerk; he never talked about himself or made promises to anyone. His house was resplendent and dazzling, but devoid of warmth. His bewitching eyes would tantalize the mind to the point of madness, but for *his* pleasure alone. His arms would twine around her bare elbows—for the sake of *his* passion. He would imbibe deeply of her body's subtle perfumes, but ever and always—for his *own* personal pleasure. In delectable horror, she would close her eyes, proudly believing that she had aroused these passions by her beautiful appearance and her boundless pride. They would gaze at each other with watchful eyes, he contenting himself with this "lovemaking," she provoking him with her flirtatiousness with Lerk.

Meanwhile, Astor was asleep inside the dark chamber, in the hypnotic slumber of an innocent child. Today was the seventh day of his mysterious experiment, which he had confided to no one. The air in his chamber was thick and heavy, and the magnetic needle in the device had ceased to tap out its enigmatic telegraphy.

It was ten o'clock in the evening. Iva had invited Lerk to supper. The large room was lit by six lamps so that every corner was visible. Fresh air streamed through the open windows, and the beautiful acacia trees in the garden were practically brimming with heavy fragrance. Iva had ceased to mention Astor at all, and Lerk, for his part, was careful not to remind her of him. There had been no sign of him for seven days; his house remained shuttered, and only the bird Kraa was hopping about on the flat roof, energetically foraging for insects. Never once did Iva call the bird over, never once did she throw a little grain on the path for him, and she even came to hate the animal that reminded her of her vanished lover. Sitting opposite Lerk, she acquiesced to his flattery and his passionate declarations of love.

"Iva, take pity on my heart and be mine. We'll move somewhere where you won't have to tend gardens or toil in nurseries. We'll go traveling, and you'll bask in the glory of my name and my love, and I in your beauty. I'm now working on a magnificent invention that will eclipse the name of Phenomén himself! Don't trust that man; he doesn't love you. You're nothing but a plaything to him. In his excess of passions, he'll even have his way with girls such as Máv," he said scornfully, pouring wine into his goblet.

"Máv, the banquet-hall arranger?" Iva exclaimed in surprise, and her eyebrows rose perpendicularly.

"Yes, Máv. She told me so herself," and Lerk recounted the familiar story, though adapting it to suit his purposes. He glossed over how she had found her way to the nobleman and his bedroom.

Prostitution by a woman was a terrible crime, and Iva almost swooned at the ugly thought of it. Her trembling fingers kneaded the fabric of her vest-front, her large eyes boring into Lerk's mendacious face. She did not want to believe that this tiny child was capable of such a terrible crime. She was still so young and had plenty of time to be with a man, and yet love had sprung out of nowhere for her, for no woman lacked for a man or was doomed to perish in solitude. A nasty suspicion filled Iva's soul, and she said passionately: "Then surely he's brought her under his spell. Máv is an innocent, after all. I don't believe it, I can't believe it," and disturbed, she set off across the room. Lerk was taken aback, thinking he would have to be more careful with his words next time.

A gentle flapping from the opened window jarred them from their thoughts. Iva went quickly to the sill and looked out into the garden. There on the path, Kraa the bird was hopping about in the lamplight in front of the house. He was pulling something white along behind him and pecking at it with his beak, trying to grab hold of it, but he could not. Back he flew to the open window, drawing their attention by beating his wings against the glass. Astonished, Iva went out into the garden and picked up the item the bird had been busying himself with so intently.

She found it to be an envelope with a wax seal and Astor's writing on it. With a shudder of foreboding, she quickly tore it open. It was her lover's last will, with a letter full of love and a plea to wake him at one in the morning on the seventh day. He gave her complete instructions for what to do and how to operate his miraculous lamp.

"Oh, my dear Iva, only love unblemished can wake me," he wrote, indicating the small chamber where she was to look for him.

A deathly pallor overshadowed Iva's lovely cheeks. Over and over, she read the letter filled with love and pleading, until she thought she would go mad. She plunged her fingers into her hair and let out a full-throated, heartrending scream.

It was already the last day, and one o'clock was long gone. Some of the lights on the bridges had already gone out, and the floodlight beams were shining more intensely. Under these white lights, she flew towards Astor's house like a woman hounded by the Furies. She raced through the wide garden and a small door in the main building out into the courtyard. Kraa flew after her, squawking merrily, for he was very fond of his master's lady friend. She stroked his outstretched wings and stood helplessly. Where to now? If the house was locked, how could she get inside? She tore at the door handle in her haste and anxiety, but it would not budge.

Round the walls she ran, her arms outstretched and grasping at the ornamental plasterwork until her fingers were raw. These minutes seemed an eternity, and she was filled with desperate fear. Floodlights as brilliant as the Milky Way fell upon the house, illuminating it from the rooftop to the foundation. This glare flooded the one open window in what she took to be a sign from the heavens. Laboriously, she clambered up the wall and dropped down into a room. Then the anxious search resumed as she called out his name.

She had no idea where to find the darkened chamber. Running from room to room along the hallways, through the passages and corridors, she could not find it. She ran out onto the flat roof and sank to her knees. The glaring floodlight shone brightly on, casting its full magnesium light on the kneeling Iva so that she looked like a saint in gloria. She pressed her clenched fists into the green moss on the roof and called upon the Spirits of the Dead to aid her. Kraa flew out of a nearby window and dropped onto her hands with a pitiful screech. He beat and thrashed his wings all about, drew himself up again, and flew to the window. He seemed to be showing her the way to go. She drew herself up at once and followed the bird. In a flash, he perched on the windowsill, and before she knew it, he had flown inside. Without any hesitation, she climbed in after him. She drew back the crimson curtain to let in the light, and the beam filled the small chamber. Astor's handsome body lay on the low divan, his fair face rigid and pallid. In the glare of the floodlight, its outlines were so ghastly that she covered her face with her hands in horror, gave a moan of the deepest anguish, and sank to the ground.

The floodlight's white glow vanished as it turned its gaze to another part of the city. She could hear the watchmen's signals on the bridge, mournful and distant as a siren song. Kraa perched on the roof's gable, hooting like a magpie. A dead silence and stillness took hold in Astor's chamber, where the needle of the remarkable device began softly ticking away again, intercepting … celestial dictation.

The Night of the Dead

Below, the river was murmuring, the waves slapping against the concrete banks and washing over the wide drafts of the boats carrying bricks and other materials for building and repairing the bridges. The spring morning was waking, with birds chirping and the fiery sunrise bursting through the heavy mists over the rivers. Everything was alive with flowers and their scents. The spreading acacia trees ran in a double line along the river, forming an avenue where locals liked to go for walks. Racemes of flowers like white canopies formed pergolas in the avenues, and the snowy petals of falling blossoms scattered onto the stone benches. The avenues, white and magnificent, swept into the distance, where they narrowed. There the trees sank into a fragrant embrace. Robustly appealing, lovers were trysting in the early dawn, proud in their attitudes and proud in their words. A man and a woman, standing on the same social footing and the same basis of equal work, who had contrived no social formulas and who had not deceived one another with false smiles. *Equality and self-sufficiency raised the woman's lovely head high,* and her eyes gazed at her companion with a frankness free of coquetry. The woman had no need to trap him out of expediency and calculation. She respected the man, admired his work, and won his love in a civilized way.

The man loved and respected her for these qualities, and he dedicated his work to her love.

Each idealized the other's every act, every thought, and every effort, life's banality impinging on neither men's hearts nor women's delicate souls. Industry, commerce, and invention: all bore the stamp of loftier ideas for the benefit of all mankind. There were exceptions, too, nasty and ugly, but they were nipped in the bud by a judgmental public that was ruthless in punishing degenerate individuals. It punished them by forced labor, which it then publicly gave its due, so compelling them to take pride in their work and shoring up their weak character. Work and its benefits were the sole motivator, as on any world. The practical Martians upheld it, exalted it, and set it on the highest throne, as was good and right. They compensated it well and paid public homage to it. With logical, calm reason, they cut the Gordian knot that binds and confounds you. *Recognition!*—

The celestial-dictation machine was likewise awaiting its hour to awaken and be recognized. For now, it was languishing in the corner of the dark little chamber, its needle stilled, its inventor reposing in the sleep of the dead. Iva was still in a heavy swoon, and Kraa had crawled off somewhere in the attic.

The entire house was engulfed in profound silence and desolation. Evening's approach was especially fast today, for the clouds rose like the mountains in the west, hurtling past one another. They churned at the horizons and gazed ravenously at the upright lightning rods of the bridges and rooftops, furiously discharging their power there and rattling the chains and huge clamping levers that formed the watchmen's boom gates. The watchmen were prepared for this furious visitor. With rubber hoods on their heads and rubber gloves on their hands, they tightened the bolts and couplings of the iron barriers. Their hammers clanged against the rails and tested how firmly they were braced. Any cracks in the bridges were carefully filled in with pitch and asphalt to seal them against the torrents of water once they came pouring from the sky.

Indeed, the greatest wealth of the Martians' world is their bridges! Every nation and every state goes on building them. They run through every province, linking at the borders to continue onward to another state, which takes them over and joins them to its own. They are this world's principal arteries, sustaining the tempo of its life! *Governments tend them, and the people cherish them,* viewing them as you do the works of your Old Masters in the art galleries. *The bridges are monuments to great men, outstanding technicians, engineers, and inventors,* and each bridge or span has a plaque depicting the likeness of its builder. Hundreds of men have died for this plaque in gargantuan labor and in untrammeled audacity. Fathers have brought their young sons here and taught them respect for the intrepid workers.

The clouds had massed directly over the bridges as if some invisible hand, full of malice and depravity, had herded them together. From their ashen tints, they hurled jagged bolts of lightning that darted down the telegraph poles like snakelings and skittered along the wire ropes straight into the river. A sharp hiss and foul foam from the murky water would accompany the dissipation of this electric power. A fish's dead body would sometimes float to the water's surface.

Darkness deepened, and dusk thickened; signals sounded, and sirens blared for miles around. The warning lights had come on, the searchlight beams lighting up the clouds and softening the lightning's dazzling brightness.

The bridges' every corner had been illuminated, the alarm signals mounted in the watchmen's sheds, and fire extinguishers lugged into place on every wall. The clock tolled the hours, pausing gravely at each electric stroke.

Iva roused herself from her deep swoon and looked around in dismay. The small, dark chamber was lit with the glare of the lamps from the bridges, the spotlights, and the flickering lightning. Astor's body lay motionless, a sepulchral expression upon his fair manly face, and Iva threw herself upon it, weeping in despair. She was crying aloud, begging forgiveness from this betrayed man, who had no idea that her heart had been turning away from him. He had worked and loved and trusted; immense pity therefore tore at her heart, and within the searing pain and shame of this knowledge, love awoke. Kissing his pallid cheek, she called to him with the tenderest names. She forgot what he had told her to do, that he had besought her to watch over him and bring him back to life with her love unblemished and his miraculous lamp. Since finding him, she had spent most of the time unconscious and squandered the rest in pointless wailing.

Remorse gripped her, paralyzed her. She was fully aware of these wretched feelings that had kept her from saving him. In mortal anguish, she seized the lamp and laid it with trembling hands against the dear head of the dead man. Yet it flickered out as soon as it came alight. With a heartrending cry, she sank onto her knees and beat her head against the ground in boundless grief. Her insides were screaming in wild pain, the blood of the Uguls surging hot and passionate to her brain, shattering her calm composure. Cursing both Lerk and Phenomén, she ran up to the white, floodlit rooftop, and stretching her white arms to the heavens, she called upon the lightning to strike her dead and the waters to swallow her whole. The heavens shuddered with the rumble of the thunder, and lightning raced madly across the metal bridges. The spotlights illumined every bolt on the bridges, lightening the watchmen's burdensome duties. And the magnesium glow fell on the desperate Iva, writhing on the flat roof.

"O God, I renounce Thee, and I call upon the name of the new prophet, born in the deep darkness of the soaring mountains, who must bring humankind a new law and to comfort the sorrowful. I call upon thee, O Unknown One, for help and salvation, and I consecrate myself to thy faith."

A fiery blaze swept across the sky from west to east, and there were horrified cries on the bridges and below. The "heavenly envoy" charged down the wire rigging directly into an improvidently moored ship. The barrels of oil she was delivering went up in flames like underbrush, and the lightning torched the ship and her cargo. The terrified screams filled Iva's heart with horror, and she retreated to the small chamber. Torrents of rain streaming down from the clouds, a disastrous cloudburst borne by the spring storm, laid waste to all the crops, obliterated the magnificent fields of flowers, and swelled the huge rivers with muddy waters so that they surged over the walls of their concrete channels. The fine embankments and the avenues of white acacias were flooded with brackish water that uprooted everything and carried it away.

Yet the suspension bridges reared in triumph over the frenzied elements. The proud spans, cleansed of dust and grit, glittered with the fiery copper and golden bronze that embellished their ornamental railings. Like large eyes, the glass plaques of the great men gleamed with mockery and scorn at the spirits of the water and the lightning. The titanic energy of the Martians' labor had stood fast against them and restrained them with the ingenious power of its spirit.

Iva was now pacing calmly back and forth. Her surging blood was subsiding like the storm outside, her practical sense coming into focus, and she began to think quietly. She had to find some other way to awaken Astor now that the lamp had failed—because her love had failed.

The only place to turn was the sorcerous Phenomén, but she knew he would never agree to resurrect his rival. Phenomén was an inscrutable man who obscured his true intentions. She could surmise his passions and their secret outbursts that flared up even in his kisses in the crooks of her elbows. Firmly, she told herself "no," and her thoughts took a different tack. There was still Lerk, Astor's hard-working and tenacious bosom friend—but a false, secretive one who hedged his words. Again, she told herself "no," and she sat at Astor's feet.

A moon rose with a huge ring that the planet's moist atmosphere had cast round about it. Iva took a long look at its bright surface. The telephone wires glimmered in its brightness, shaking off the dewy drops of rain. With light footsteps, Máv was hovering small and tiny above them, like a white cloud spun from the river's vapors, approaching Astor's home. Horrified, Iva stared at the white apparition, waiting to see what the girl would do. She recognized Máv, the banquet-hall arranger, impugned by Lerk's lying lips and bewitched by Phenomén's eyes. Iva set herself proudly and haughtily against her, arms crossed over her bosom as she waited.

Máv entered with a sweet song of the Homay, the enchanting mountain folktale that had once set Lerk's heart trembling. She sang of both love and forgiveness, and of forgiving her lover's infidelity. She vaulted lightly up to the window and stood at Astor's head. She then began to sing again, and Iva's heart grew hard at her song. Máv sang of the beds of strangers, lamenting that Astor's was cold and dead, that it no longer gave warmth, that his heart had grown cold without the ardent kisses he might have expected from his faithless mistress. Máv had come to revive him with the glowing caresses of the hopeless love that had driven her toward another man. She had hoped to warm herself in his bed, and yet she found it so cool and chill.

At first, Iva thought she would pounce on her and throw her off the roof straight into the river. Yet the moonstruck are untouchable, and woe to the hand that harms them. Iva was now coming to understand Máv's "sin" of which Lerk had accused her. She was sorry for the poor girl, felt love for her, and dared not wake her, waiting instinctively to see what would happen next. Máv went on singing her sweet lullaby of love, stroking Astor's pallid cheek, brushing his shoulders and arms with palms warmed by her breath.

Round the bed she went in a circle, all the while in search of something and all the while singing the native songs of her distant homeland. Iva, her heart pounding with anxiety and hope, pressed the extinguished lamp into Máv's outstretched hands. Máv joyfully took hold of it, thrice circled it over her head, and the lamp brightened with a violet flame.

"Máv, Máv, have mercy, Máv," cried Iva in a muffled voice, sinking to her knees. Máv circled the lamp around Astor's head, all the love hidden in her tender, girlish heart fluttering toward him, calling him to life in the name of Love.

Iva stared intently into his closed eyes. She could penetrate the glazed lids, seeing every vein and every eyelash quiver. In a trembling voice, she called his name and asked forgiveness for his spurned love. And behold, his great and kind-hearted eyes suddenly opened and came to rest on Iva's pupils with inexpressible tenderness. She cast herself upon him and sobbed till her lovely body was shaking. Máv left the same way she had come. Warmed by her act of love to rescue a loving heart, she traced her way back along the telephone wires until she vanished on the bridges in the distance.

Zagara City

*T*he capital of the Taverian Empire, beautiful and ancient, was shrouded in morning fog when Lerk stepped out of his light vehicle at its gate. He wanted to walk through its grand streets and lose all thought of Iva in the urban bustle, for she had abandoned him so pitilessly at their last dinner and sent no word of herself since. He was affronted and plotting revenge. The city of Zagara was going to help him.

The sun was slowly rising, and as it emerged from the mists, it first dried the dew-dappled rooftops and the wooden pavement of the streets. Electric vehicles were coursing silently down the roadways, dropping off the mail as well as the night watchmen, who were changing shifts and returning to their homes. All the windows were opening joyfully to welcome the rising sun, and from them came the sound of singing and cheerful conversation. Quiet reigned over the metropolis' promenade, soundless. No transit lines crisscrossed the city or endangered its pedestrians. In the broad, splendid avenues, lanes were set aside for electric vehicles. One led into town and the other away from it. The sidewalks and the median were claimed by the public. The street traffic yielded to the community, in stark contrast to the way it is done on your world.

Railroads, warehouses, factories, all of these lay beyond the city, and vehicular conveyances made transportation simple and easy.

No foul smoke or fumes choke the city, since every home's furnace and stove is heated by electricity. The houses are only one story tall, so the sun can get through to the ground-level apartments and rooms. Martians love the sun, its brightness, and its light. They seize avidly upon every ray of sunlight by day and revel in electric light by night.

Lerk admired the marvelous colonnades of bronze and copper streetlamps polished to a golden hue. The great curving lamps hung like huge flowers on their chains. The variously tinted glass lamps set in the arms of the candelabras looked like immense jewels that would glow in every size and color by night.

The *House of the Mystic Arts* on the main avenue caught his eye. It was constructed of milky glass and enclosed within a large garden. Its frame was made of iron, so the glass walls could be shifted freely about. Inside, thick curtains that cut both the glare of the sun and the evening light from the streets were drawn over the walls. On the façade of the house was the emblem of the arcane arts in white and golden stucco: two crossed triangles centered on a large eye pierced by an arrow. Lerk did not contemplate mysticism or the occult sciences; he was too practical and too much in love with a beautiful woman to care what the arcane symbol meant. He knew only the cult of the glass building where he was an initiate; under its ceiling, he could hope to find some slight comfort in the arcane arts and perhaps also a suitable instrument for his revenge.

He pressed the electric doorbell, and the portcullis was lifted open before him. His path took him through a pleasant, shady garden to a small table spread with various journals, where he sat down. Several men and women at other nearby tables were reading intently. They were poring over literature on the spiritual arts, the women positively lapping up the colored letters. Lerk smiled at seeing the women hunched avidly over the illustrated brochures, and Iva's pretty face arose in his mind. No, she did not concern herself with mysticism; she only stirred men's passions while offering nothing in return.

Perhaps if she were more deeply grounded, like these women, she would not cheat on her lover or play so recklessly with other men's hearts. And that was exactly why she must be punished! Igo Phenomén probably had some coup de grâce in mind for her, but Lerk had to stay one step ahead of him; he had more right to her than the nobleman, who was only toying with her. She had not brought the proud minister's work to a standstill, nor had she thwarted his ambition as she did the wretched engineer's and the chemist's. How many weeks had gone by with Lerk doing no work, flitting from place to place like the sleepwalking Máv? But all he did was wander off to foreign cities, while that poor girl went straying over rooftops.

Angrily, he stacked the journals, set a paperweight on them to keep the wind from blowing them away, and looked out into the garden. Two young girls strode towards him and sat down at his table with courteous smiles. One put a bouquet of white spring violets on the table and graciously suggested he take a few stalks. Her large, brown eyes looked searchingly into his face, and her tender, red-lipped mouth addressed him with a sweet smile, "Let no beautiful woman grieve you, sir, for she shall fade like these flowers and leave no trace behind."

He bowed in silence and asked why she should say such a thing to him. "Anything may be said in the House of the Mystic Arts, for others can read your thoughts. You ought to leave your reminiscences at home before entering the mystery of this place, otherwise, they'll settle onto your eyes and mind like shadows; and you'll understand nothing of the hidden phenomena, and then what face shall the masks assume? It saps your soul and your energy," the girl said gently and with kindness.

"You're right. I can clearly sense this in myself, too. I haven't done any work for weeks now, and that's why I've come here to draw comfort. Do you know what the program is today?" Lerk asked, his pale face blushing slightly in the presence of the two girls.

"There are no programs here. How can anyone know what is concealed in the hidden phenomena and what face the masks will assume? Four new mediums have just been trained and are making their first public appearance today. They're said to have astounding abilities. They are women of various ages, have submitted to all the rites and trials, and have been permanently admitted to this house."

"How I envy them, Lucia," said the other girl.

"Why?" Lucia asked with a warm smile. "I should not wish to be in their place. Their art forbids them to love a man, and they must live chastely and not start families. And that is too severe a religion. I would rather love and be loved," and her fiery eyes rested long and meaningfully on Lerk's face. He blushed even more and felt a stir of pleasure. He gave the proffered flowers a courtly kiss and returned the fiery look. He felt happy and content, his somber memories receding in the young women's presence, and he began to hope that maybe he could be happier with another woman, one whose love was straightforward, than with Iva, whose conquest demanded such arduous efforts. His companion was pretty and sweet, dark-haired and dark-eyed. Her white lace gown was becoming, and the blue beads on her neck, hanging down to her waist, lifted slightly on her full bosom, which was breathing deeply. Her white teeth, big, strong, and healthy like the beads, sparkled every now and then in a hearty laugh. With a smile like that, he thought it odd that she would come to the House of the Mystic Arts, for it did not accord at all with her outward appearance or behavior. But who could ever fathom the heart of a woman or the depths of the sea? And Lerk did not like to think too hard about women. A woman was not to be puzzled over like chemistry. Her name was Lucia, she was pretty and cheerful and sensible, and that was enough for him.

Her companion was just the opposite, with blonde hair and blue eyes that she kept lowered, with a dreamy expression to them. She wore a pink silk jerkin of a peculiar cut that covered her neck up to her ears. Black pearls dangled from her tiny earlobes, real black pearls set in gold that made weird reflections in her blonde hair and blue eyes. The pearls were long, like teardrops, and a red gemstone cluster glittered at the rounded tip of each one. They were truly striking and looked lovely on her sorrowful face. Cara knew this and how to use them flirtatiously. But she remained sad and sulky, and while Lucia was happily enjoying herself, Cara kept on leafing through journals and jotting things down in her notebook.

The gong struck thrice, startling them, and Cara turned deathly pale.

"We must go now, Lucia. Please don't leave me alone in the auditorium. I'm very nervous and afraid of the apparitions," Cara pleaded fearfully.

"You ninny, we won't be alone today; this gentleman will accompany us, won't he?" Lucia asked in such a cheerful and kindly voice that Lerk bowed silently in token of his assent, and he escorted them inside with pleasure at once.

They went inside the glass building, and on entering the vestibule, they had to submit to a minor formality. First, they took off their shoes and put on rubber slippers. They received white, veiled hoods for their heads, and the women had to take out and hand in all their hairpins. Thus "prepared," they made their way into a great hall, where they had to pass through the smoke of fragrant herbs rising from a brazier at its center. A little girl dressed in white kept throwing herbs on the fire, turning them with an iron spade so they would all be thoroughly heated. Their delicate scent wafted all the way up to the glass ceiling. Cara held Lucia's hand anxiously as her friend smiled cheerfully and passed through the white smoke. Lerk followed close behind them, and they were now inside the main hall of the building.

It was an auditorium. The curtains were still down, and the light was low. Blue lamps burned here and there, and like great campanula flowers, they marked off the loges. Visitors could sit wherever they pleased. Each loge accommodated three people and consisted of a long plush seat with a small round table before it. The pencils and papers on it were for anyone to use. Each loge was separate from the next one and closed off with a light curtain. Lerk let the girls go ahead as he drew the curtains completely shut. On the wall of the loge were regulations that had to be followed to the letter, lest everyone submit to unseen peril from which there was no escape.

When there were two men and a woman in the loge, the woman had to sit between them, and vice versa. Only three were permitted inside, neither more nor less. No loud talking was allowed! When someone was alone in the garden, that person had to make the acquaintance of other visitors to complete the requisite number. That was why the two girls had introduced themselves to Lerk. He was glad they had done so, for in the presence of women, the phenomena were more subtle and much more beautiful than in the presence of men. Cara pulled her veiled hood down over her ears and lapsed into a deep silence. Lucia fiddled impatiently with a pencil and frequently leaned out of the loge, surveying the other visitors. Suddenly she gave a start and yanked the curtain shut.

"What's gotten into you, Lucia? What is there to hide from?" Lerk asked, the hint of an unpleasant surmise curving his mouth into a scoff.

"Be quiet, he's here—Igo Phenomén!" Lucia scolded him in an anxious whisper, and she yanked Lerk back as he tried to see for himself. His pale face grew even paler, and his eyes flashed in the loge's gloom.

"Lucia, are you afraid of him?"

"Yes, he is cursed! Terrible things happen in his presence, but he turns them to his own advantage and can command unknown influences to serve his purposes. That's why he's so dreadfully powerful, and no one can stop him from coming here, since he's under the protection of every country. It's better to hide from him, and any beautiful woman who goes near him will be sorry. He bewitches her with his snakelike eyes, but he never loves her. Then she ends up incapable of love, however madly she longs for it. That sacred emotion is not given to an unworthy heart," Lucia said slowly and carefully so Cara would not hear her.

Iva sprang to Lerk's mind, and an uncontrollable hatred for this man all but choked him. He knew that Phenomén had toyed with Iva and stolen her away from him, whose intentions toward her were sincere, since he loved her with a grown man's love and passion. Deep down, he suspected Phenomén of snatching Iva away from him, supposing that must be why she was in hiding. Lerk had seen the letter in her hand, and he believed it to be from Phenomén, who must have lured her out of the house. Then Iva disappeared, and he had seen no more of her since then. Astor's house was still shuttered, and Iva's gardeners were carrying on with their work without their mistress. The two neighboring houses were desolately empty; his good friend and that friend's mistress had both disappeared, and no one knew where they'd gone. That was why Lerk had come here today, to this mysterious place where he might be told where to look for her and how to exact his revenge.

Lucia shrank into a dark corner, pulled Cara close, and they both began to pray fervently. Lerk fell back into his old thoughts and paid the girls no more mind.

All the lights in the auditorium and in the loges went out. The curtain on the stage was parted, the small space there lit by a single lamp glowing cozily and intimately with a garnet-hued light. A small altar stood at center stage, flanked by couches where women dressed in white lay reclining. One of the mediums stood up and walked over to the altar. She raised her bare arms over the lace cover, and a white flower slowly sprouted from its surface. It grew and grew, unfolding its buds, which quickly developed into broad, beautiful calyces, and for several minutes it delighted the spectators with its exquisite loveliness.

Then it slowly began to droop, its petals falling off and catching on the lace of the altar cloth. The woman then whipped at them with a violent motion, using the light fabric of her garment, until they had flown all over the auditorium. They were joyfully snatched up by hands that shot out from the loges. Cara caught two and placed them on the table before her.

Suddenly, a large fireball flew off the stage and straight into Phenomén's box. Lucia clutched Lerk's hands convulsively and anxiously pulled Cara closer. "He's started with his magic now," she whispered low in Lerk's ear. Another sphere flew out, much smaller, and fell on the stage directly on top of a sleeping medium, who gave a weak cry and stood up. Then like the sleepwalking Máv, she rose lightly, languidly, from the sofa; and with deep-sunken eyes and her arms outstretched, she moved toward Phenomén's loge. Her delicate limbs were quivering constantly, and her tiny feet were treading as carefully as if walking over boulders, though the floors were thickly carpeted.

"Oh, no, she's giving way before Phenomén's strong will and his bewitching eyes. The poor medium!" Lucia whispered, leaning against Lerk's shoulder.

"What can he do to her in this place?" Lerk asked angrily.

"Nothing, but he'll drain her of all that's best in her. Most of all, he wants to take over her abilities for his own gain," Lucia replied.

"She's lovely," Cara whispered, pointing at the medium as she passed their loge with hushed steps. Lerk fixed his eyes eagerly on her face, which was lean, almost gaunt, and white as alabaster. Her dark eyebrows and lashes made her look even whiter. Lerk had not seen such delicate skin in a long time, and his heart throbbed with admiration at her classically beautiful face. He suspected that Phenomén was therefore luring her in order to make her his own. That old hatred, man's jealous selfishness and resentment of any other who would snatch up the most beautiful woman with impunity, so contorted his unattractive face that he could not control his anger, and he flung his small binoculars at the medium, striking her squarely on the forehead. The girl sank down with a cry of pain. In an instant, the lights came up in the auditorium, and the girl was carried away by the theater attendants. No one knew where the binoculars had been thrown from or who had done it, but Lucia looked in horror at the chemist's contorted face and clasped her hands in fear.

"What have you done? Why did you do that?"

"I didn't want her to belong to that damned fellow."—

The lights went out again, and the show went on. The injured medium lay back down on the couch, and when Cara saw her, she broke into silent weeping.

"Why are you crying?" Lerk asked anxiously, gently stroking her hand.

"Oh, sir, look at how my husband, my dearly departed husband, is sitting beside her."

And indeed, the figure of a vigorous young man was sitting at the medium's feet, looking sadly into the auditorium.

"Your act of violence has constrained him, and he refuses to leave his medium, the one you struck, else he would have come to me in the loge," said Cara reproachfully, and she began to moan softly.

Conscience and compassion stirred in Lerk. He understood that he had meddled with the influences and injured three beings with a single blow. The medium physically, Cara with sorrow, and her husband by depriving him of the few kisses he had brought from beyond the grave to his forlorn wife. Suddenly understanding her grief, he quietly sought her pardon. "Forgive me, Cara, forgive me, how can I make amends?"

"You cannot!" Lucia broke in vigorously, "be quiet and don't interfere!"

"I won't come here with you again if you can't behave properly toward the mediums," the aggrieved Cara childishly reproached him. He kissed her hand, still pleading in a whisper for her forgiveness.

A large figure appeared onstage and thrust his arm menacingly at the audience. Suddenly all the curtains in the loges were pulled shut, and only through the openings in them could attendees look at the stage. The figure continued to threaten and throw swords into the audience. The swords had phrases inscribed upon them in various languages, and Lucia quickly read them as they sailed past their loge.

"War with Russia." "German hostility." "France's defensive war." "England's navy." "America to the rescue." "The fall of Austria." "The liberated nations." "Independent states." "Cheap slogans." "Subversion," *etc*. Lucia couldn't read them all and couldn't stop laughing.

"The whole of Earth is at war, those wretches!" Lerk grinned as Cara alone kept on softly crying. The swords were dropping away somewhere, vanishing into the auditorium like scattered smoke. But the spectators took no interest in them; on Mars, these kinds of weapons had long ago been put aside, and they were unknown to the younger generation. Only their elders would speak of them now and again, as if of old and forgotten tales. Phenomén smiled ruefully at the pompous phrases of their bloody neighbor, Earth. A Martian, he had other and newer weapons for bloodletting, as Lerk was soon to learn.

Phenomén knew it was Lerk who had injured the beautiful girl—the medium—and snatched her away, just as Phenomén had snatched Iva from him. He thought, just like Lerk, that his rival was hiding the girl and keeping her prisoner for himself.

The figure vanished from the stage, and the lovely medium rose from her sofa. As before, she once again began to roam delicately and cautiously across the proscenium, descended slowly into the audience, and with a casual air approached the loge where our friends were sitting. Cara stopped crying and watched as the visitor drew closer; Lucia threw aside the curtains, and the medium came to a stop near the opening to the loge. The handsome young man embraced Cara, who hung on his neck with a cry of unspeakable happiness. His lips came to rest on hers in a silent kiss.

Both Lerk and Lucia watched the lovers' embrace, their hearts trembling and eyes brimming. The chemist's defiant heart thrilled with pity, and his mouth involuntarily cried out the name of his lost Iva. The painful memory loomed once more before his mind's eye, and he lost all interest in what he was looking at. The fair medium bent down and kissed him on the forehead.

"Have hope!" she said softly before turning away. Then she withdrew her hand tenderly from Cara's husband's and left quietly. After her departure, the three fell silent and became absorbed in their emotions and their memories.

A red drop of blood fell upon Lucia's white dress, then a second, a third, and a fourth.

Lerk's head was leaning against the wall, bent toward her shoulder, and he did not notice the drops of blood falling from his nose. Neither did Lucia, absorbed in her own thoughts, her eyes fixed on the stage, where still other manifestations were in progress.

The three mediums were seated around the altar, their hands joined in a magnetic circle. The golden cauldron on the altar was gleaming faintly in the light of a single electric lamp. The mediums were "brewing" curative herbs and filling small bottles with them, then distributing the bottles to the audience. It was the most cherished and admired of the mediums' curative arts. Lucia reached eagerly for the bottle that was deposited in her lap by an unknown and unseen hand. Lerk received nothing, and neither did Cara. "You have your hate and Cara her love; you each have what you have made for yourself," said a voice from the stage.

All at once, a sharp explosion blew the cauldron apart, sending shards into the air, scattering the small altar across the stage. The mediums swiftly retreated behind a wall of asbestos to escape the danger as the flammable substances began to pool upon the stage, shooting in all directions like rockets.

A glorious fountain began to spurt up to the ceiling of the glass house, reflecting off the palace walls like mirrors, and a spectacular cluster of colors cast reflections of light on the mediums, who began to dance around the fountain.

An unfamiliar music and the song of a thousand voices began to pour in unseen waves from somewhere, accompanying the women's concerted dance and bewitching the listeners. It was a gorgeous harmony of lights and tones and sweet symphonies such as the Martians did not know how to create.

The women wept in their yearning to capture these chords, and the men sat forlorn, listening to these sounds that showed Earth's advantage over their poverty. They had no knowledge of these "voices of bridges," born in the first glimmers of music and poetry; only Máv would heed them, but practical minds passed right over these hidden tones of nature!

The fountains subsided, the lights came on, and the curtains in the loges began to open. The audience quietly departed, and the auditorium began to empty out. Lerk left with the girls, covering his nose and mouth with a kerchief. Lucia was looking for a conveyance to leave in, for she did not want to walk down the street in her bloodied dress. Cara would not be parted from her, so moved was she by the reunion with her husband. So Lerk offered to drive them in his vehicle and telephoned to order it from the city gate where he had left it. His bleeding continued, drop by drop, and not even the mediums' medicine that Lucia had received could stanch its flow. Lerk drained the entire bottle, but to no avail. Lucia was dismayed, suspecting that the pale chemist had been injured in some mysterious way, and thinking with horror of the nobleman. If he had injured Lerk, he must have had his reasons. But what could they be? Surely there was a woman involved, for Phenomén was not dangerous otherwise. On the contrary, he was high-minded, charitable, and generous, but he passionately desired any love that he could not have. Beautiful women would elude him, and he did not care for ugly ones. Lucia suspected that he was capable of a crime of passion for a beautiful woman, but she could not ask Lerk about his dealings with Phenomén and the cause of their antagonism. The young man was mortified because his bleeding kept him from talking. He had to hold the kerchief over his mouth with one hand and drive the car with the other, so that he could not show his companions the courtesies that won women's hearts.

In a quiet street, in front of the little house where Lucia lived, he stopped the car and helped them both alight. They exchanged warm and friendly goodbyes, promising to visit him soon to check on his condition. Lucia pressed his hand with both her palms and gave him a heartfelt look. He smiled at her tenderly and clutched to his heart the flowers she had given him in the garden when they met. She blushed and went quickly inside. They were both still nodding to him as the vehicle moved silently off, like a bird, over the wooden pavement.

Fateful Inventions

*T*he huge aerodrome was neatly raked and swept, and the lanterns hanging from the high struts of the hangars were festooned with green branches. Aeronauts crossed back and forth in rubber suits reminiscent of those worn by divers. Light vehicles came and went, women and men getting out of them to enter the nearest air station, where they would buy tickets for their flights. In the distance, the artery of life surged across the bridges, coursing over them day and night.

Air travel relieves the crowded trains, charting its flight paths through the ether and using electricity to intercept the aerial currents and invisible tracks that the planes glide along so securely and effortlessly. A precisely calibrated electrical current charges the plane with magnetism as a ray of electricity locks onto the airship's magnetic underside. There is no potential for deviation from an aerial trajectory or for collisions between two aircraft. Aeroplane 4 follows its flight path as precisely as Aeroplane 10 and all the many others.

At each air station, the delicate magnetic instruments softly tap out their telegraphy, directing the inbound aircraft in their flight, drawing them homeward by a force harnessed to the laws of nature and mutual affinity.

Just as lightning and storm clouds are attracted to lightning rods and mountaintops, so is each plane drawn to its mother station.

The airway is free from error or disruption, its electric discharges harnessed by the indomitable Martian, whose bridges proudly reach and whose pathways boldly soar across the rippling waves of air. Even the clouds obey, clustering on the mountaintops at his command, generating artificial lakes that produce salt. The globe's interior was long ago depleted of its salts, for the Martian reconstituted them into other compounds, and Mars's bosom yields no more of them. Yet he no longer needs natural salts to maintain his skeleton, fortifying his bones instead with… artificial limestone. (Not in your sense of the word on Earth, of course.)

Aeroplane 8 roared, shook its outstretched wings, and dropped into a huge wire net, like a bird shot down from the sky. It swelled slightly, like an ocean wave, and then settled. The peculiar electromotor ran for a moment longer, whirring and letting out a long whistle. Wireless telegraphy signals followed, recording the precise hour of its successful approach and landing.

From the netting, the arriving passengers descended the spiral stairs, gazing curiously in all directions. They were foreigners. Attendants escorted them courteously and telephoned to order vehicles, which drove quickly out to meet them right on the tarmac.

The foreigners took off the rubber coats and hoods they had put on for their flights and quickly went about their business.

An old woman, about fifty Earth years old, was turning about anxiously amid all the other people, looking for someone and not knowing which way to go. One of the attendants inquired solicitously what she might be looking for. She answered in an unfamiliar language, showed him a piece of paper, and again began to turn about and look at all the men milling around the aerodrome.

Suddenly she ran toward the air station, and before anyone knew it, she had shattered the mirrored panel over a telephone, the proud invention of the mighty Lektona. People ran up and surrounded the woman. She was waving her arms in exasperation, spouting a strange language, and railing against the telephone. At last they understood what had happened, which had already sent the merry throng into peals of laughter on many occasions.

The magical telephone panels were displaying the heads and faces of various strange creatures that were nothing like the faces of the Martians. The scientists were puzzling over it, examining the mysterious apparitions, but the people went on laughing heartily.

It was so comical when an engineer would telephone the laboratory for some materials and the panel would show the face of an antediluvian animal like something from a museum. Or a writer would call the printer for a manuscript or some proofs and instead of his interlocutor, a face strange and unfamiliar to Martians would appear. A woman telephoned distant relatives with news of the death of a family member, only for the deceased's face to appear in the panel. Clearly, other forces were taking control of the sensitive panels and manipulating their circuitry. Sometimes there was great laughter, sometimes great weeping, always depending on the circumstances. Something similar must have happened to the old woman in using the telephone to make her go and smash the panels with a vengeance wherever she found them. She was finally pacified, put in the nearest vehicle, and taken to the Foreigners Office, where they followed protocol with her. She paid for the broken panel, railing all the while against modern inventions.

Whooshing like darts tossed through the air, the aeroplanes would land in the taut nets and then lift off from them, ejected by the tensed meshwork like a rocketing cannonball.

The passengers, however, have felt neither the landing nor the ejection, for the interiors of their small cabins are lined with silken netting where they hang like flies in a spiderweb.

The netting sways in accordance with the plane's speed, so that even a flight lasting several hours does not tire the seasoned traveler. It is the timid and the squeamish who take a train across the bridges or opt for a boat.

Lerk was driving home in his vehicle when Aeroplane Number 5 zoomed overhead. It was of a design he had once worked on for several years and made him a tidy sum. He smiled from pride in his labor, and he greeted the aircraft silently with a tip of his hat. So now he had another invention in train, but his unrequited love had brought him to a standstill. Maybe things would be better now, maybe Lucia would take the ungrateful Iva's place and calm his erotic desires.

It was impossible to work on Mars without the love of a woman: no delicate hands to touch his instruments, no fair head to lean over his drawing desk, and no astonished eyes to peer into his mysterious laboratory. Ah, and how he had longed for this; he wanted to hear a cry of admiration, and he pined for the words, the recognition of beloved lips; but during the long nights, all his arm might embrace was the cold tube of the telescope where the tiny Máv had once appeared to him only to vanish again. Yet his pale face longed to be embraced and kissed by a beloved woman's ardent lips.

Oh, Lucia, how I'll adore you if you will only give me your love, a woman's pure and healthy love! His bleeding continued its incessant dripping at the same intervals. Lerk's senses were reeling, confusing Lucia with Iva, one face mocking him, the other smiling at him with young and budding love.

The vehicle was swerving with his erratic driving, his arm drooping from fatigue and his eyes heavy as lead.

Somewhere in the distance, the sweet songs of the Homay were in the air as the mountaintops glistened with white, silver snow, shrouded in mists where the dear faces of his parents and siblings were fading away. The fine, straight road leading out of Zagara City went curving around a small grove, which the chassis finally crashed into under its own momentum. The electric apparatus was still thrumming faintly, but Lerk's passionate heart beat for the last time. Lucia's sweet memory haunted his dying brain and slowly stanched his quickening blood.... Phenomén's act of murder was a covert one, and the handsome, wealthy nobleman could carry on unmolested.—

Iva was again up and about, her train thrown proudly over her left elbow, for Astor, brisk and hale again, was striding beside her with an enthusiastic smile on his lips. The manicured gardens were delightfully fragrant and the well-stocked nurseries with their vases of bouquets still open, but no longer did Iva concern herself with them. She left everything to the shopgirls, devoting herself to looking after Astor and keeping a jealous eye on his *celestial dictation* device. Oh, how many times she'd wanted to shatter it with a water funnel, as she had the vases in the nurseries when Phenomén's eyes had hexed them, but she feared her beloved Astor's wrath. She paced and skulked about like a cat, eager to pounce on the magnetic needle and even plunge it into her heart if that would only distract him from yet another mad experiment. Astor, however, adored his invention and was always dusting it, moving it from one corner to another, and copying out the peculiar writing. "What did the magnetic needle pick up, Astor? Read it to me!" Iva begged, kissing him on the forehead.

"Oh, darling, it's a secret," Astor laughed in his playful way.

"I don't want there to be any secrets, I just want the truth as it is," Iva pouted, kicking at the stand with her foot.

"I have to be discreet about other people's affairs. My needle has picked up a dispatch between two governments on Marconi's telegraph. After all, they still have state secrets!" and Astor burst into a friendly laugh that infected both Iva and Kraa, who was back to squawking merrily around his masters.

"Then don't give it away, you'll be arrested for treason!" Iva laughed merrily. "Tell me what else you've picked up," she demanded eagerly.

"I haven't deciphered it yet, for these Earthlings have a mysterious, enchanted code." Astor placed the panel on the table, and Iva leaned over it curiously.

"Then how are you going to decipher it? Who can read it? I'll look up Professor Mleno. He's invented some new form of writing, so maybe he can find the key to this mystery as well," Iva offered.

"Darling, this isn't human script but an ethereal one!"

"*Ethereal script!*" Iva exclaimed after him, not understanding the meaning of this invention.

"Yes, ethereal script! The future language of every inhabitant of every planetary system. Such 'celestial dictation' devices must be installed in all the observatories, so that we can communicate with other heavenly bodies. I'll give the invention of 'celestial dictation' to another man on another world, but he must be fully worthy of it!"

"Don't let him have it unless he loves a woman!" Iva cried in passionate protest. "I was so anxious in my love for you as I followed your doings in that dark chamber. I was mad with grief when I couldn't wake you. Demand no less of him than this, or I'll crush and trample him to pieces," Iva sobbed, hanging passionately on his neck.

"You're right, my darling, it must be sanctified by love. I'll wait until I find such a man, but there's little true love on planet Earth. Romances between men and women there have little to do with purity and much to do with sensuality."

"Then don't give it to anyone, ever!"

"But I must work for progress," Astor countered, taking her hands.

"Sanctify it with love if it's to be of any use to anyone!" Iva insisted defiantly.

"I promise, Iva, that I'll only give it to a man whose love for a woman is like mine for you," Astor said solemnly, and he kissed her on the eyes and her slanted eyebrows.

The wonder-working lamp was lying on the table before them, and Iva tried in vain to make it light up in her hands. Astor himself was surprised at this, and warily, he scrutinized her face closely. With a guilty conscience, Iva shivered under his gaze and tried to divert both her mind and his attention toward other things. Astor was stubborn, however, and would not let a matter drop once he had taken it up in his mind.

"Why won't it light up for you like it used to? How did you revive me?" he asked several times, jealously watching her pale lips.

"There was a storm just then. An electrical surge was turning on all the lights, and it must have turned on your lamp, which is how I woke you. It's not my fault that it won't turn on now. It isn't saturated with my persona fluidum.[1] That was how you put it once," she said in passionate protest, her rebellious temper began to stir dangerously, hitherto chastened by her deep concern for the beloved being she had found once again.

"Then take it in your hands, breathe on it, and it will light up again!" he urged with a child's good-natured confidence.

Iva felt that if his confidence was shattered, all was lost. No words, no reassurances, no amount of persuasion would restore the blissful sense of security that was the glory of Astor's heart. It was pure, idealistic, and Iva would be sorry if her image should be tarnished within it. Astor would be quick to leave her and find another woman who lived up to his ideals. He was even willing to leave for other worlds if only he could reach the great goal he had set himself. His pulse throbbed to a different beat. Driven by neither passion nor sensuality, he worshiped only science and bowed only to love—yet since each one inspired the other, he merged them both into a single whole. Together, labor and love saturating the soul: this was the law that sustained his ideals and drove his efforts. Science and labor did not leave his mind drained as was the case with other scientists; his heart was not desiccated by austere learning or unkindness, for his science was love, and love was science to him. Iva stood on the same level as his inventions, sometimes even higher. He would not shunt her aside with a scientist's severity; on the contrary, Iva would strut jauntily about in his laboratory right alongside the boldest idea firing up his mind just then. Iva was aware of all this, and she would rather have

---

1. A theosophical concept akin to *prāṇa* (life force, spiritual energy) in various forms of Indian thought.

died than have lost this throne that would be the envy of any woman. For that reason, her heart fluttered with uncertainty and anxiety lest her flirtations be exposed.

She was afraid of both Lerk and Phenomén. She, the proud Iva, who walked with her train thrown proudly over her left elbow, who could gaze boldly into Phenomén's bewitching eyes, who could listen with disdainfully raised eyebrows to Lerk's fiery words! Her pride now lay in the dust, and the one support that had sustained her devoted love was tottering. Oh, sin, how thou dost weaken!

The telephone's electric bell started to jangle so madly that Astor and Iva were startled. They turned toward the wall at the same time, and the magic mirror over the phone box provoked a horrified scream. It was showing Lerk's pale, dead face, along with the car on the curve of the road leading away from Zagara City.

"Lerk, for God's sake, what's happened to you? Where have you been all this time?" Astor burst out, horrified. However, the dead face gave no answer, and there was only the sound of the telephone's furious jangling. Astor took the headset and put it over his ears. The messenger of the dead was calling to tell him that he had found his friend dead on the highway and that he would bring his body home.

Iva, though she had been startled to death, could have shouted for joy. So Lerk was dead, and her love had been saved from peril.

Calmly, she began to prepare to receive the body, for piety demanded that the deceased should be borne from his last abode to his final resting place. Since Lerk had kept no servants at home, Astor took the liberty of burying his dead friend himself. The mournful cortège arrived an hour later along with the physician, who diagnosed brain hemorrhaging—caused by an injury.

"A mysterious one!" he emphasized, for this injury was not visible. Only his nostrils were crusted with blood; his clothes also showed signs of the bleeding, and a soaked kerchief was found at the bottom of the car—but there was no sign of struggle anywhere.

They laid out Lerk's body in the airy room where he had last dined with Iva and betrayed his friend. A tear in his eye, Astor took his miraculous lamp and illuminated the head of his dead friend.

The telephone rang a second time, so shrilly that Iva cried out in horror. Above it, in the magic panel, there appeared the name of … Phenomén!

"Igo Phenomén, he murdered him, damn him!" Iva cried passionately.

"Why should he have?" asked Astor, startled.

"Out of jealousy!" Iva imprudently exclaimed.

One word is sometimes all it takes for a person to condemn herself. Say it just when love is at its most alert, and you'll hear its death-cry and collapse, and no kiss can reawaken it. Though you lay the most beautiful feelings at love's feet, it will not accept them; it has been betrayed and tormented unto death. In vain, you may promise and call it by the tenderest of names; it will remain as mournful as a tomb. It may forgive, but it will no longer love you.

But say unto an ailing man, one who trusts you implicitly, a single comforting word to assure him that he will recover, and you shall see light spark in his faint pupils, and how eagerly he will hang on the promises of your lips! The illness shall be broken, thrust aside to the wall by the bed, and the patient will revive in your presence.

Iva grasped her misfortune, and she clenched her fists in mad defiance. More words appeared on the magical panel, where Phenomén accused Iva of betraying Astor and murdering Lerk:

"I killed Lerk because he stole Iva from me!" The vicious Phenomén was taking revenge for the lovely gardener's rejection, and for the curses she had heaped upon him.

Astor stood white, blanched, and deathly pale. He then kissed Lerk on his treacherous brow, looked silently and sadly at Iva, and left the room.

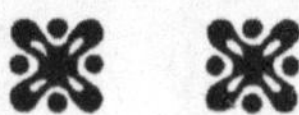

Malaya Vurpur

Summer was blooming in all its glory. The opulent rosebuds were bursting forth in the secret corners of the night, and the mystery behind the birth of the flowers' invisible beings suffused the air with stupefyingly heavy melancholy. How sublime to walk alone in the hidden paths of the gardens, to listen to the voices of Earth, and to incline one's heart to the places where holy solitudes beckoned. Their calls into the night were like psalms sung over ruined temples and hearts that have been stilled. Departed loves would call, weeping, their arms reaching through the evening dew within a shower of stars. Faint echoes of the celestial horizons keened mournfully over lives wasted and the neglect of any single day. A single hour is enough to bring down the proud edifice of hope.

The temple of human love is of the finest and most delicate design, and woe betide all who enter there with ambition in their hearts. You must lay all that comprises human life upon its sacrificial altar.

Iva wanted everything but gave little. The handsome, good-hearted Astor had laid at her feet all that poured forth from his spirit and heart, and on her passionate lips he had built the pride of his labor and his manly ambition. Yet in her feminine coquetry borne of pride and anger, she brought down all that love's delicate fingers had built, and buried it....

Iva was an ordinary woman, and that was why Astor had turned away, painfully wounded and affected by this ordinariness, and his heart died because his love had abandoned the noble ideal of womanhood.... Iva responded like any ordinary woman! Deep within the flowering gardens, a painful cry rang out, and among the rose bushes it fell. Iva sat there on a narrow seat, searching ... herself; her analysis of her own heart was ruthless in its judgment, laying low her proud self that had been so adored and loved.

No longer was she Iva, lovely, proud Iva, for all that was left of her was the pitiful shell of the expired essences that had once dazed Astor's heart.

Her arms had lost the enchantment of any embrace, her mouth was tainted with lies, and her heart had been so open that it could welcome three men at once. The gate had slammed shut behind them and clanged with Lerk's demise and Phenomén's vile accusation.

Another cry rose through the blooming garden, a cry of wounded pride and the knowledge of irredeemable loss.

Iva stood up and proudly threw her train over her left elbow. She entered the house, drew a bath, and wrote out her last will. Among the perfumes she was pouring into the bath, she discovered the flask given her by Phenomén at the feast of talents as a reward for her beautiful flowers. Only today did she carefully unwrap it from its silken pouch and examine it searchingly. The golden vignette had letters of cast white porcelain: *Malaya Vurpur*. "Poison," Iva exclaimed ruefully. "Oh, that damned Phenomén! Perhaps even then, he knew our destinies and rewarded us accordingly, honoring both the present and the future. He knew that one day I'd be determined to take my own life and wouldn't know what weapon to choose, so he gave it to me in advance. He seated the messenger of the dead on his left and me on his right; oh, what symbolism as he showed me the contrasts in human lives as he meant to drink of my own with his demonic power. Did he suspect my fate, of which he himself was the instrument? Oh, that villain! If only I could give you this very elixir of death you have given me and then clasp you in a deadly embrace."

Malaya Vurpur is a poison that takes three hours to work its effect on the body.[1] It is painless; intoxicating hallucinations lurk within it, and even after death, it keeps the soul mesmerized for decades. When lovers take it, it lingers upon their lips for a hundred years after death.

Iva let out a mad laugh and threw back her proud head. The electric clock struck the hour slowly, drawing it out: nine. At that moment, the telephone rang, and Iva turned deathly pale. She was now afraid of this device and terrified of its electric bell. Yet she resolutely threw on her robe and left the washroom. The magical tablet was blank, but the telephone continued to jangle implacably. With closed eyes, she put the headset over her ears and shouted "hello!" loudly and angrily. *"I'll be there at midnight—Phenomén!"* The headset rattled, dangled briefly on its cords, and suddenly came crashing down. Iva was laughing hysterically.

The comfortable bedchamber was aglow in the faint, milky light of the two-branched candelabra hanging over the nocturnal bed. Iva's pink robe lay there as she finished combing her hair, carefully weaving white acacia blooms into her tresses—*Phenomén's* favorite flower. A crystal

---

1. "Malaya Vurpur" (Czech *Malaja vurpur*) is an invented name. "Malaya" sounds like the Russian feminine singular adjective for "little," and "vurpur" evokes the Czech *purpur* (purple [color]) phonetically.

chalice filled with white wine stood on the table, next to a large vase likewise filled with acacia flowers. The heavy scent suffused the room, deadening her lively mind and preparing her heart for its moment of truth.

Her hair was styled, and her weird eyebrows were covered by a silver netting from which hung two large, white pearls that dropped to her temples just at the ears. Iva donned the pink robe, slipped on a pair of velvet slippers, and her attire of death was complete.

She emptied the Malaya Vurpur into the wineglass and took a small sip. She did not want to be fully conscious. She would be Phenomén's in the heavy fog and stupor of the poison, until he died along with her, for he would drink of love and death along with her from this single chalice. He had killed her love, and in return she would kill him with love as well.

The rich and handsome nobleman had a fatal desire for her love, so she would give it to him, but at the cost of his life.

Perhaps he would divine her intentions, as he did everything, and cheat death once he had drained her of all the fleshly passion she was about to bestow upon him. But with this passion, she would draw him into a fatal toast. Her half-breed blood was seething in her veins, and her passionate Ugul blood demanded the passion and death of the one who had set her aflame.

The clock struck eleven as Iva turned down the bed and scattered acacia blossoms over it.

In the distance, the bridges were rumbling, those high-flown bridges that men and women had built in their proud ambition to labor and be admired. Their architects were dead, leaving only their panels in the electric lamp-glow to mock the death that had cast them from their towering, gigantic work's vaulted arches. So many men had died there for planetary progress, and so many women had chosen a voluntary death over a spurned love. Astor's slab will be placed there too, lit by the floodlights, because he built watchmen's huts and fit their walls with fire extinguishers.

Iva would be at rest in her deadly dream by then, within her marble sarcophagus.

No artistic embellishments by loving hands shall grace its lid, nor shall the messenger of the dead bring greetings or remembrances from those left behind.

Phenomén's body shall rest at her side, for together on a single deathbed shall they lie. Martian custom called for lovers to be buried together for eternity. Astor's heart will turn away from her in disgust, and that will make it easier for her to forget…

When the clock struck twelve, there was the sound of rapid and hurried footsteps on the staircase. The bedroom door opened, and upon its threshold emerged Igo Phenomén, as handsome and proud as a conquering god. Iva shuddered, and her weird eyebrows stood up perpendicularly. Yet Phenomén could not see their menacing uplift, for they were concealed by the silver netting. Tall and proud, Iva received the nobleman with her lips compressed, her train thrown over her left elbow. Her individual fragrance came streaming from every pore with the sudden upsurge of her soul, and Phenomén was intoxicated with this perfume, which he loved to the point of madness. Yet he spoke not a single word!

Imbibing her pale face's dark, beautiful eyes, he hung her bare elbows around his neck, pressed his handsome, chiseled lips to hers, and drank…. He drank a full draft, his every limb trembling with the arousal of this desire so long denied him. Iva sank in his arms, her senses thrilling to the burning love of this exquisite man. To live or to die—in his presence, it was all the same, as she understood with all her senses, and she surrendered herself to him in fatal ecstasy, in the erotic surging of her race's blood…. She handed him the full chalice of wine, her pupils widened, eagerly awaiting his reaction and whether he would suspect this drink of death for what it was. He drank half, and she finished the rest herself.

"*Malaya Vurpur!*" he cried aloud and gripped her in his passionate arms. "I shall remain upon your lips for a hundred years! You have broken the curse … with a kiss lasting a hundred years, you shall redeem what the curse has denied me…."

In her horror, she thought of Lerk, his murder, and his curses; she howled through her death rattle and collapsed onto the bed.

Phenomén embraced her with still greater passion, pressed himself to her dying body, his deep inhalation pulling her lips to his twitching mouth; and like a vampire, he was absorbed into her evanescing soul.

He now lay in the sweet embrace of a death granted him by this beautiful woman with her deadly chalice. He had taken everything from her … both death and love!

The Song of Máv

The three sarcophagi were riveted firmly shut, covered with pitch, and the smooth marble lids bore the golden inscriptions of the departed sleepers. The coffins stood close together and had identical golden letterboxes. Slender palm trees stood at both Lerk's and Phenomén's heads, their branches dropping down to the sarcophagi lids.

At Iva's head were roses, that same rosebush she had destroyed in a fit of rage when the nobleman's eyes had hexed them, and that Astor had named after Phenomén.

Astor had illumined the buds with his miraculous lamp, and they blossomed with a violet-scarlet hue, though their base tone was a deep crimson. The velvety petals retained the wondrous illumination, and at night they would glow over the sarcophagus with the subdued fire of violets and the sweet intimacy of love, breathed into them by a loving heart.

Over Phenomén's sarcophagus, on the day of his death, there appeared two phantoms, the heads of a man and a woman, each one's lips touching the other's in a fatal kiss.

In those days, Máv would approach in a hypnotic trance, sing them psalms, and fall into a swoon, sinking down to the marble pedestals. The messenger of the dead would bear her away and curse the name of Phenomén....

Astor had locked himself away in his dark chamber and given himself over to his invention. He had deciphered Earth's "ether script," devised a new alphabet, and recorded the symbols of the new telegraphy.... And with that, "celestial dictation" had its own form of writing, which was his secret.

After a long period of mourning, he once again smiled the happy smile of a man working for ideals. Higher ideas now guided his lonely heart, and in the pride of his labor he left human grief behind....

A huge telescope now stood permanently on the flat roof of his home, and a map of the heavens was stretched taut between two brackets.

These were the nights of summer's glory when nothing would disturb a quiet recluse and bold laborer. A hatch-door led from the dim chamber to the roof, where the "celestial dictation" device was placed and covered with a white cloth to prevent light and air from damaging the magnetic needle. The glass cloche covering it had to be kept in the shade. The magnetic needle was so sensitive that it would even tremble at his approach if his heart were aquiver with curiosity. When his mind was empty and desolate, drained of painful memories, the needle would stand stock-still on its delicate axis, but when his soul was seized by a scientist's enthusiasm, the needle would also tremble and the bell-glass cloche softly chime through the vibrations of aerial waves that it spread.

She worked, loved, and remembered—at his side!

Astor's tender glances would caress her, his love as a proud worker adore her. Oh, it was well that Iva was already at rest in eternal dreaming, for she would surely have been crushed with wild jealousy over Máv. She had become a dangerous rival, for she was wholly devoted to him and belonged to him alone.

As Astor slept in his hypnotic trance, the needle faithfully captured what his unbridled soul dictated to it. It had transcribed the entire history of nearby Earth, of its all-out war and the dizzying changes taking place in every nation. Science was reviving there, casting off obsolete dogmas and combining with the faith of the people. The torches of progress lit the universe's dark expanses and called to the stars for help. Earth's redeemers from every age were rising in a new religion, and men's hearts crying out to them, tortured and bloodied by the wretchedness of materialism.[1]

The stargazers and the scientists were expanding Earth's horizons and waiting for Mars to come within sight of their telescope lenses so that they might triumphantly signal their greetings to their proud colleagues....

Meanwhile on Mars, the great scientist slept on in his hypnotic trance, watching Earth's new trends and perfecting his "celestial dictation." All the observatories had one now, and Astor's name soared over his world in a triumphant march of proud labor and recognition.

In the spirit of self-sacrifice, he intended to bring it to other worlds, and nearby Earth was to be the first in line if it could produce a man worthy of it, one who could fulfill the conditions set by his departed mistress. Astor was faithful and true even in death, and he wanted never to break his promise to Iva. He would never give his invention to a man who did not love and honor women, because only the heart influenced by a woman's love is capable of and open to the higher worlds in conceiving a high ideal. "Celestial

---

1. This image recalls Czech author Julius Zeyer's short story "Opálová miska" ("The Opal Bowl," 1882), in which a sage's young acolyte is allowed to meet Socrates, Buddha, Jesus, Joan of Arc, and Jan Hus, humanity's redeemers.

dictation" was Astor's purest ideal, one that he raised proudly even over his departed mistress' sarcophagus…. Her body had long since been at rest in the sleep of the dead, but his invention was blazing a trail of immortality for the good of humanity and the innermost planets orbiting the Sun, and it was overcoming the vast distances that separated the worlds from each other. "Celestial dictation" had its interplanetary telegraphy, its future ethereal script!

Little Máv had intercepted it on the bridges as it sang in the electric current and magnetic breath of Earth.

She would come and rouse the handsome Astor with a song of his script, rousing him with bygone love and the sweet songs of the Homay, summoning him from his deathlike fog:

> *Lightly I go, O my lord, like a dream*
> *Borne on love's sorrow and night's soft stream*
> *By starlight and thousands of spotlights*
> *The prayers of the Homay my only song,*
> *To clouds in the night, I rise along*
> *The eyes of the dead in these heights now strong.*
>   *O my lord, why grieve when thou couldst sing?*
>
> *Hark, how the bridges pulse with life's refrain*
> *Their great plaques shine bright in night's domain*
> *Their courage through toil and strife not in vain….*
> *In thousandfold radiance, their lights are aglow*
> *Quickened by Martian souls' ardent breath*
> *As the bridges give voice to a low requiem,*
> *I weave through my longing a symphony for them*
>   *O my lord, why grieve when thou couldst sing?*
> *I come now to banish thy deathly dream.*

And Astor awoke, proud and triumphant, illumined by the miraculous lamp as she shone it upon his head with the tenderest solicitude. He then clasped her in a rapturous embrace and kissed her on her lowered eyes.

"Máv, Máv, wake up!" … This was how they would wake each other! She brought him back to his work, and he her … to sweet memories.…

"O my lord, you are my brother in sleep and I your sister in wakefulness. Tell me, where are we to meet on that day I fail to awaken you, when I shall be as one struck dead?"

"On Earth! For I have found a being there to whom I can give my work, and you … your sweet, budding poetry. Oh, Máv, how magnificent is a man's work when crowned by a woman's poetry!"

BIBLIOGRAPHY

Adamovič, Ivan and Jaroslav Olša, Jr. "Czech and Slovak SF." September 6, 2021. In *The Encyclopedia of Science Fiction*. Edited by John Clute, David Langford, Peter Nicholls, and Graham Sleight. https://sf-encyclopedia.com/entry/czech_and_slovak_sf.

Adamovič, Ivan, Ondřej Neff, and Jaroslav Olša, Jr. *Slovník české literární fantastiky a science fiction*. Prague: R3, 1995.

Adamovič, Ivan. "Psaní jako kosmická telegrafie. Po stopách první ženské autorky české fantastiky." In *Měsíčník Host: literatura, kultura, společnost* 39, no. 8 (October 2023): 78–85.

Alpers, Hans Joachim. "Germany." September 13, 2021. In *The Encyclopedia of Science Fiction*. Edited by John Clute, David Langford, Peter Nicholls, and Graham Sleight. Gollancz. https://sf-encyclopedia.com/entry/germany.

Anonymous. "List of German-speaking science fiction authors." Second.wiki.com website. Accessed January 8, 2022. https://second.wiki/wiki/liste_deutschsprachiger_science-fiction-autorinnen.

Anonymous. "Zofia Urbanowska." In *Encyklopedia.naukowy*. https://encyklopedia.naukowy.pl/Zofia_Urbanowska. Accessed January 24, 2022.

Arbes, Jakub. "Newton's Brain" [From "Newtonův mozek" (1877).] Translated J. J. Král. In *Clever Tales*: 134–204. Edited by Charlotte Porter and Helen A. Clarke. Boston: Copeland & Day, 1897. https://archive.org/details/clevertales00unse/page/122/mode/2up?q=Arbes.

Arbes, Jakub. *Newton's Brain*. [From "Newtonův mozek" (1877).] Translated by David Short. London: Jantar, 2024.

Beneš, Pavel. "Elegantní jednoplošník Rapid bratří Čiháků—první letadlo české konstrukce." In *Vynálezy a pokroky* (1913). Reproduced at: https://www.bejvavalo.cz/clanky.php?detail=892.

Besant, Annie and C. W. Leadbeater. *Thought-Forms: With Fifty-Eight Illustrations*. London and Benares: The Theosophical Publishing Society, 1905. https://archive.org/details/in.ernet.dli.2015.213512/mode/2up.

Besant, Annie. *Odvěká moudrost: tresť učení theosofického od Annie Besantové*. [From *The Ancient Wisdom* (1897).] Translated by Pavla Maternová. Prague: Hejda a Tuček, 1920. https://kramerius5.nkp.cz/view/uuid:20ef09f0-4a16-11e4-8113-005056827e52?page=uuid:791b8590-5e57-11e4-8fe2-5ef3fc9bb22f.

Besant, Annie. *The Ancient Wisdom: An Outline of Theosophical Teachings*. London: Theosophical Publishing Society, 1897. https://archive.org/details/in.ernet.dli.2015.217385/page/n3/mode/2up.

Bezděk, Robert. "Antroposofie a její vliv na spiritualitu v českém prostředí." Master's thesis. Brno: Masarykova univerzita, 2008. https://is.muni.cz/th/f9m8t/Rigorozni_prace.pdf.

Blavatsky, H. P. "Stars and Numbers." *The Theosophist* (June 1881). https://universaltheosophy.com/hpb/stars-and-numbers/.

Brubaker, Jesica. "Early Female Authors of Science Fiction/Fantasy." San Diego State Library website. https://library.sdsu.edu/scua/new-notable/early-female-authors-science-fictionfantasy-0.

Čapek, Karel. *R.U.R. (Rossum's Universal Robots): A Fantastic Melodrama*. [From *RUR* (1920).] Translated by Paul Selver. Second edition. Garden City [New York]: Doubleday, Doran & Company, Inc., 1928. https://archive.org/details/rossumsuniversal0000kare/page/n9/mode/2up.   [First edition: Garden City: Doubleday, Page & Company, 1923.]

Carlson, Maria. "Fashionable Occultism: The Theosophical World of Silver Age Russia." *Quest* 99, no. 2 (Spring 2011): 50–7.   https://www.theosophical.org/publications/quest-magazine/fashionable-occultism.

Chayka, Kyle. "A Short History of Martian Canals and Mars Fever." *Popular Mechanics* (September 28, 2015). https://

www.popularmechanics.com/space/moon-mars/a17529/a-short-history-of-martian-canals-and-mars-fever/.

Clute, John. "Lucian." August 5, 2021. *The Encyclopedia of Science Fiction*. Edited by John Clute, David Langford, Peter Nicholls, and Graham Sleight. https://sf-encyclopedia.com/entry/lucian.

Clute, John. "Theosophy." August 5, 2021. *The Encyclopedia of Science Fiction*. Edited by John Clute, David Langford, Peter Nicholls, and Graham Sleight. https://sf-encyclopedia.com/entry/theosophy.

Comenius, John Amos. *Labyrinth of the World and the Paradise of the Heart*. Translated by Count Lützow. New York: E. P. Dutton & Co., 1901. https://archive.org/details/labyrinthofworld00come.

Crossley, Robert. *Imagining Mars: A Literary History*. Middletown [Connecticut]: Wesleyan, 2012.

Cultura.pl. "Andrzej Żuławski, 22.11.1940–17.02.2016." https://culture.pl/en/artist/andrzej-zulawski. Accessed September 2, 2024.

Czaplińska, Joanna. "Does Czech Science Fiction Have a (Feminine) Gender" [From "Má česká science fiction (ženský) rod?" (2015).] Translated by Carleton Bulkin. *Journal Hélice: Critical thinking on speculative fiction* 8, no. 1: 9–20. https://www.revistahelice.com/revista_textos/n_32/Hélice%2032%202022%20Primavera-Verano%20GZAPLINSKA.pdf.

Czaplińska, Joanna. "Má česká science fiction (ženský) rod?" In *Sedm statečných a spol. Próza psaná ženami v kontextu české literární kultury*: 58–71. Edited by Ivo Říha and Jiří Studený. Pardubice: Univerzita Pardubice, 2015.

Duchamp, L. Timmel. "Science Fiction and Utopias by Women, 1818–1949: A Chronology." Webpage. http://ltimmelduchamp.com/essays/chronology.html.

"Edison's Perfected Phonograph." Illustration. *Harper's Weekly: Journal of Civilization* 32, no. 1642 (June

9, 1888): 415–6. https://archive.org/details/sim_ harpers-weekly_1888-06-09_32_1642/page/416/ mode/2up?q=dictation.

Fekete, John. "Science Fiction in Hungary." *Science Fiction Studies* 16, no. 2 (July 1989): 191–200. https://zh.booksc. eu/book/27021900/659d93.

Figes, Orlando. *Natasha's Dance: A Cultural History of Russia.* New York: Metropolitan Books, 2002.

Fischer, William B. *The Empire Strikes Out: Kurd Lasswitz, Hans Dominik, and the Development of German Science Fiction.* Madison: University of Wisconsin, 1984.

Flammarion, Camille. *Haunted Houses.* [From *Les Maisons hantées* (1923).] Translated by E. E. Fournier. New York: Appleton, 1924. Available for digital loan at: https://archive. org/details/hauntedhouses00flam/mode/2up.

Flammarion, Camille. *Les Maisons hantées.* Paris : Ernest Flammarion, 1923. 1978 edition: https://archive.org/details/ camille-flammarion-les-maisons-hantees/Camille%20 Flammarion%20%20-%20Les%20Maisons%20Hantees.

Flammarion, Camille. *Urania.* [From *Uranie* (1889).] Translated by August Rice Stetson. Boston: Estes and Lauriat, 1890. https://archive.org/details/uraniaflam00flamuoft/page/2/ mode/2up.

Flammarion, Camille. *Uranie.* Illustrated by Gambard and Myrbac De Bieler. Paris: C. Marpon et E. Flammarion, 1889. https://www.gutenberg.org/ebooks/52933.

Flournoy, Théodore. *A Case of Somnambulism with Glossolalia.* [From *Des Indes à la planète Mars* (1900).] Translated by Daniel B. Vermilye. New York: Harper & Brothers, 1900. https:// wellcomecollection.org/works/s6afce8h/items?canvas=5.

Flournoy, Théodore. *Des Indes à la planète Mars: étude sur un cas de somnambulisme avec glossolalie.* Paris: F. Alcan, 1900.

Flournoy, Théodore. *From India to the Planet Mars: A Case of Multiple Personality with Imaginary Languages.* [From

Des Indes à la planète Mars (1900).] Translated by Sonu Shamdasani. Princeton: Princeton University Press, 1994.

Goodrick-Clarke, *The Occult Roots of Nazism*. Wellingborough: Aquarian Press, 1985.

Gyimesi, Júlia. "The Problem of Demarcation: Psychoanalysis and the Occult." *American Imago* 66, no. 4 (2009): 457–70. http://www.jstor.org/stable/26304942.

Halloran, William F. *The Life and Letters of William Sharp and "Fiona Macleod". Volume 3: 1900–1905*. Cambridge [UK]: Open Book Publishers, 2020. https://doi.org/10.11647/OBP.0221.

Hauser[ová], Eva. "Science Fiction in the Czech Republic and the Former Czechoslovakia: The Pleasures and the Disappointments of the New Cosmopolitanism." *Science Fiction Studies* 21, no. 2 (1994): 133–40. http://www.jstor.org/stable/4240328.

Herec, Ondrej and Miloš Ferko. *Slovenská fantastika do roku 2000*. Bratislava: Národné osvetové centrum, 2001.

Hudáková, Andrea. *Organizace československého spiritistického hnutí*. Ph.D. dissertation. Prague: Univerzita Karlova, 2012. https://theses.cz/id/3t3nsd/STAG84213.pdf.

Jókai, Mór. *Tales from Jókai*. Translated by R. Nisbet Bain. London: Jarrold & Sons, 1904. https://www.gutenberg.org/files/37286/37286-h/37286-h.htm.

Kennon, J. L. (pseud. of [Mabel J. McKean]) *The Planet Mars and Its Inhabitants: A Psychic Revelation by Eros Urides (A Martian)*. [n.p.]: [self-published], 1922. https://www.gutenberg.org/ebooks/563.

Kepler, Johannes. *Somnium*. Translated by Tom Metcalfe. *The Somnium Project* [website]. https://somniumproject.wordpress.com.

Killheffer, Robert K. J. et al. "Mars." March 15, 2021. In *The Encyclopedia of Science Fiction*. Edited by John Clute, David Langford, Peter Nicholls, and Graham Sleight. https://sf-encyclopedia.com/entry/mars.

Kozák, Jaromír. *Spiritismus: zapomenutá významná kapitola českých dějin*. Prague: Eminent, 2003.

Krejčí, Karel. *Česká literatura a kulturní proudy evropské*. Prague: Československý spisovatel, 1975.

Krome, Frederic, ed. *Fighting the Future War: An Anthology of Science Fiction War Stories, 1914–1945*. New York: Routledge, 2012.

Kurlander, Eric. "Between Weimar's Horrors and Hitler's Monsters: The Politics of the Supernatural in Hanns Heinz Ewers's Fiction." In *Zwischen Popularisierung und Ästhetisierung: Hanns Heinz Ewers und die Moderne*. Edited by Barry Murnane and Rainer Godel: 229–56. Bielefeld: Aisthesis Verlag, 2014. https://www.academia.edu/11270771/Between_Weimars_Horrors_and_Hitlers_Monsters_The_Politcs_of_Race_Nationalism_and_Cosmopolitanism_in_Hanns_Heinz_Ewers.

Lagalisse, Erica. *Occult Features of Anarchism: With Attention to the Conspiracy of Kings and the Conspiracy of the Peoples*. Oakland: PM Press, 2018. https://pdfs.semanticscholar.org/86e6/0190c370252ff641232b3dc00226c34488f4.pdf?_ga=2.184398562.535237158.1642101446-233759003.1642101446.

Laßwitz, Kurd. *Na zemi a na Marsu: román*. [From *Auf zwei Planeten* (1897).] Translated by K. V. Telč: Emil Šolc, 1904. https://kramerius5.nkp.cz/view/uuid:a733a3b0-00a3-11ea-af21-005056827e52?page=uuid:fa7924f9-3811-4451-9d08-99a10e23cd45.

Mayer, Sandra. *Oscar Wilde in Vienna: Pleasing and Teasing the Audience*. Leiden: Brill, 2018.

Nakonečný, Milan. *Novodobý český hermetismus: Druhé, přepracované a rozšířené vydání*. Prague: Eminent, 2009.

Neff, Ondřej. *Něco je jinak*. Prague: Albatros, 1981.

Neff, Ondřej. "Příliš mnoho samotářů." In *Tři eseje o české sci-fi*: 10–32. *Puls*, vol. 5. Prague: Československý spisovatel, 1985.

Ockerbloom, Mary Mark, ed. "A Celebration of Women Writers: Pre-1950 Utopias and Science Fiction by Women: An Annotated Reading List of Online Editions." https://digital.library.upenn.edu/women/_collections/utopias/utopias.html#1950. Accessed August 30, 2024.

Olša, Jaroslav, Jr. "Bibliography of Czech Science Fiction in English Translation: A Supplement." *Foundation* 44 (Winter 1888/89): 50–4.

Plass, David. "Historie Martinistického řádu v Čechách." Bachelor's thesis. Prague: Univerzita Karlova, 2014. https://dspace.cuni.cz/bitstream/handle/20.500.11956/70807/130138747.pdf?sequence=1.

Proietti, Salvatore. "Science Fiction in Continental Europe before the Second World War." In *The Cambridge History of Science Fiction.* Edited by Gerry Canavan. Cambridge: Cambridge University Press, 2019.

Putna, Martin C. *Václav Havel: duchovní portrét v rámu kultury 20. století.* Prague: Knihovna Václava Havla, 2011.

Pynsent, Robert. *Julius Zeyer: The Path to Decadence.* The Hague: Mouton, 1973.

Seidl; Jan et al. *Od žaláře k oltáři: emancipace homosexuality v českých zemích od roku 1867 do současnosti.* Brno: Host, 2012.

SF2 Concatenation. "German Science Fiction up to 1945." *Concatenation.org* [website]. Updated October 9, 2015. http://www.concatenation.org/europe/german_science_fiction_before_ww2.html.

Simsa, Cyril. "Bibliography of Czech Science Fiction in English Translation." *Foundation* 40 (Summer 1987): 62–72. https://www.proquest.com/openview/5c376233fab5b62c8f12efcaf5f2ab71/1?pq-origsite=gscholar&cbl=1816914.

Simsa, Cyril. "Josef Šimánek (1883–1959): Czech Pagan Fantasist." *Wormwood: Literature of the Fantastic, Supernatural and Decadent* 7 (Autumn 2006): 37–51.

Stableford, Brian and David Langford. "Moon." August 2021. In *The Encyclopedia of Science Fiction.* Edited John Clute,

David Langford, Peter Nicholls, and Graham Sleight. https://sf-encyclopedia.com/entry/moon.

Studnička, František Josef. *Luňan Hvězdomír Blankytný Broučkův host v Praze roku 1891*. Prague: P. Čech, 1892.

Taylor, MacNeil Christian. "Disqualified Knowledge: Theosophy and the Revolt of the *Fin-de-Siècle*." Bachelor's thesis. May 23, 2013. Middletown [Connecticut]: Wesleyan, 2013. https://citeseerx.ist.psu.edu/viewdoc/download?doi=10.1.1.343.7630&rep=rep1&type=pdf.

Tomei, Christine D. "On the Function of Light and Color in Andrej Belyj's Petersburg: Green and Twilight." *The Slavic and East European Journal* 36 (1992), no. 1: 57–67. https://doi.org/10.2307/308349.

Weiss, Jan. *House of a Thousand Floors*. [From *Dům o tisíci patrech* (1929).] Translated by Alexandra Büchler. New York: CEU Press, 2015.

Weiss, Sara. *Journeys to the Planet Mars, or Our Mission to Ento*. New York: The Bradford Press, 1903. https://www.gutenberg.org/ebooks/61253.

Zach, Aleš, ed. "Zmatlík a Palička." December 25, 2018. *Slovník českých nakladatelství 1849–1949*. https://www.slovnik-nakladatelstvi.cz/nakladatelstvi/zmatlik-a-palicka.html?fbclid=IwAR0jo7yvFWArurasG-jDevoVZu49lhHS0ZyntR7oqGwHN1dp18p22g89o4o.

Žarnay, Jozef. "Science Fiction from a Dusty Shelf: A Short History of the Fantastic in Slovak Literature to 1948." Translated by Cyril Simsa. *Science Fiction Studies* 23 (Part 1), no. 68 (March 1996). https://www.depauw.edu/sfs/backissues/68/zarnay68.html.

Żuławski, Adam. "The Origins of Polish Sci-fi and the Legacy of Jerzy Żuławski." *Culture.pl* (November 29, 2020). https://culture.pl/en/feature/the-origins-of-polish-sci-fi-the-legacy-of-jerzy-zulawski.

WOMEN OF SPECULATION:

Women Authors of Speculative Fiction in Central and East Europe Prior to 1950

The following list of "speculative fiction" extends from gothic, folkloristic, and utopian narratives to spiritualist and science-fiction ones, including tales written for children or early aviation enthusiasts. From the mid-nineteenth century and into the twentieth, popular, essentially realist stories often included one or more fantastic elements (viz various works by the French writing duo Erckmann-Chatrian). Since then, this approach has sometimes been called "slipstream," but it has been around for a while.

I have tried to be as inclusive as possible in constructing this list, but I have not yet identified any Albanian, Bulgarian, Greek, Macedonian, Serbian, or Slovak women authors of speculative fiction in this period. Any suggestions for additions are welcome. For a broader survey of women who contributed to these genres, see Mary Mark Ockerbloom's *A Celebration of Women Writers: Pre-1950 Utopias and Science Fiction by Women*.

This list is sorted by author. The authors are sorted according to the date of each one's first known "speculative" work, and their respective works are listed chronologically.

Mostowska, Anna Olimpia (née Radziwill) (ca.1762–1810) [Poland (Russian Empire)]. Gothic horror writer.

> Mostowska, Anna Olimpia. *Matylda i Danilo* [Matylda and Danilo]. In *Moje rozrywki* [My Pastimes], vol. 1. [n.p.], 1806. Translated from Stéphanie Félicité, Comtesse de Genlis.

> ———. *Zamek Koniecpolskich* [The Koniecpolski Family Castle]. In *Moje rozrywki* [My Pastimes], vol. 2. [n.p.], 1806.

———. *Nie zawsze tak się czyni, jak się mówi* [You Don't Always Do As You Say]. In *Moje rozrywki* [My Pastimes], vol. 3. [n.p.], 1806.

Żmichowska, Narcyza (pseud. Gabryella) (1819–1876) [Poland (Congress Poland)]. Gothic horror writer.

Żmichowska, Narcyza. *Poganka* [The Heathen] (1846). Multiple editions including Kraków: Nakładem Krakowskiej spółki wydawniczej, [1930]. Translated into English by Ursula Phillips as *The Heathen: A Novel* (Ithaca: Cornell University Press, 2012).

Urbanowska, Zofia (1849–1939) [Poland (Russian Empire)]. Fantastic literature writer.

Urbanowska, Zofia. *Atlanta, czyli przygody młodego chłopca na wyspie bezludnej* [Atlanta, or the Adventures of a Young Boy on an Uninhabited Island]. Kyiv: Księgarnia i Skład nut H. Lechelina, 1893. Also published in Kraków: Księgarnia Gebethnera i Spółki, 1893.

von Bernstorff, Fanny (Countess) (1840–1930) [Germany]. Children's fantasy writer.

von Bernstorff, Fanny. *Alfred und Nanny bei den Zwergen. Eine lustige Geschichte aus dem Reiche der Heinzelmännchen* [Alfred and Nanny with the Dwarfs. A Funny Story from the Brownie Kingdom]. [n.p.], 1895.

———. *Franz und Minchens Abenteuer* [Franz and Minchen's Adventure]. [n.p.], 1899.

———. *Miki, das Mondkind. Ein Märchen* [Miki the Moon-Child. A Fairy Tale]. [n.p.], 1910.

———. *Was Großmütterlein erzählt* [What Grandmother Told]. [n.p.], ca.1910.

Kryzhanovskaia, Vera Ivanovna (pseud. J. W. Rochester) (1861–1924) [Russia]. She is especially well known for her pentalogy *The Magicians* and her trilogy *The Realm of Darkness* but authored many other novels influenced by her spiritualist beliefs. She was widely translated into European languages.

She resided in Paris 1886–90; and also in Petersburg, Warsaw, Narva, and Tallinn per the Moshkov Library (az.lib.ru). She was decorated by the French and Russian academies of sciences. She was married to S. V. Semenov, president of Society for Psychical Research in St. Petersburg. She died of tuberculosis.

For biographical sources, see (1) Nolde, L. *Вѣра Ивановна Крыжановская (Рочестер): опыт характеристики*. St. Petersburg: Iekateringofskoe pechatnoe dielo, 1911. (2) Maguire, M. "Ghostwritten: Reading Spiritualism and Feminism in the Works of Rachilde and Vera Kryzhanovskaia-Rochester." In *Modern Language Review* 106 (2011), part 2: 313–32. (3) During 2022–3, a now-vanished Portuguese-language blog published a longer profile called "Abre um chamado" (Open a Call) at http://abreumchamado.blogspot.com/2013/10/vera-ivanovna-kryzhanovskaia.html. A study of Kryzhanovskaia's publishers may also yield additional helpful biographical, historical, and cultural context.

Many of the texts below, as well as biographical studies, are available in Russian at the Moshkov Library: http://az.lib.ru/k/kryzhanowskaja_w_i/. These citations come from Worldcat.com, Bibliothèque russe Tourguenev (tourguenev.fr), and the Moshkov Library. Titles have been listed in the order of first known publication in any language. Dates in parentheses after the initial title (with tentative English translation) come from the Moshkov Library. Publication dates estimated by catalogers are square-bracketed. Searches of the national libraries of France (catalogue.bnf.fr) and Russia (nlr.ru) may yield new titles, editions, and translations. Various titles are available as e-books from major retailers. Translations of translations abound. The list below is not complete.

Kryzhanovskaia, Vera Ivanovna. *Épisode de la vie de Tibère* [Episode in the Life of Tiberius]. Paris: E. Dentu, [1885/1886].

———. *Два сфинкса : романъ въ 2-х частяхъ* [Two Sphinxes: A Novel in Two Parts] (1892). Part I: *Любовь Царевны* [The Tsarevna's Love]. Part II: *Клятва*

Мага [The Magician's Oath]. St. Petersburg: Tovarishchestvo, 1916. Riga: M. Didkovskii, 1927. Riga: M. Didkovskago, 1930.

————. *Месть еврея* [The Jew's Revenge] (1892). *La vengeance du juif, drame social en 5 actes et 8 tableaux* [The Jew's Revenge: A Social Drama in Five Acts and Eight Tableaux]. Transl. [Marius Boisson, Lucien Ricaille]. Paris: P.-V. Stock, 1905. *The Revenge of the Jew* [English]. [n.p.]: World Spiritist Institute, 2023. *Месть еврея* [Russian]. [n.p.]: Litagent "Sed'maia kniga," 2013.

————. *Сим победиши! Hoc signo vinces! : roman* [By This Be Victorious! A Novel]. St. Petersburg: V. V. Komarov, 1893.

————. *Торжище брака* [The Wedding Feast] (1893). Editions include: [n.p.]: Vita, 1994.

————. *Рекенштейны : романъ, Часть I, II* [The Rekenshteins: A Novel; Parts I, II] (1894). Part I: *Габриэль* [Gabriel']. Part II: *Лилия* [Liliya]. Riga: N. Gudkov, [n.d.] [n.p.]: Ripol klassik, 2003.

————. *Царица Хатасу* [Tsaritsa Khatasu] (1894). St. Petersburg: V. V. Komarov, 1896. *Královna Hatasu : román ze života starých Egypťanů* [Czech]. Prague: E. Beaufort, [1906]. *Царица Хатасу : романъ* [Russian]. Riga: Academia, [1930/n.d.]. *Hatasu: A reinha do Egito* [Brazilian Portuguese]. [n.p.]: Editora do conhecimento, 2009. *Tsaritsa Hatasu* [Russian]. [n.p.]: TBRUGRAM, 2018; Book on Demand Ltd., 2018.

————. *Геркуланум : роман из древне-римской жизни* [Herculaneum: A Novel of Ancient Roman Life]. St. Petersburg: V. V. Komarov, 1895. Riga: Izd. M. Didkovskago, 1930.

————. *Варфоломеевская ночь : романъ въ 3-хъ частяхъ* [St. Bartholomew's Massacre [Paris, 1572]: A novel in three parts]. St. Petersburg: Komarov, 1896.

————. *Заколдованный замокъ : романъ* [The Enchanted Castle: A Novel] (1898). St. Petersburg: Komarov, 1898. [n.p.]: Kondus, 1995.

————. *Желѣзный канцлер древняго Египта : роман в 2-х частях* [The Iron Chancellor of Ancient Egypt: A Novel in Two Parts]. St. Petersburg: Glavnago upr. udelov, 1899. Riga: Izd. M. Didkovskago, 1931.

————. *Адския чары : оккультный романъ* [Infernal Charms: An Occult Novel]. Riga: Izd. M. Didkovskago, 1900, [1925?]. *Адские чары* [Russian]. Simferopol': Biznis-Inform, 1993. The Moshkov Library gives a 1910 publication date.

————. *Жизнь и смерть : сказка* [Life and Death: A Tale]. St. Petersburg: V. V. Komarov, 1900.

————. *Нахэма: средневековая легенда* [Nakhema: A Medieval Legend] (1900). St. Petersburg: V. V. Komarov, 1900. Riga: Izd. M. Didkovskago, 1932.

————. *На рубежъ : нарвское предание* [On the Frontier: A Narva Legend]. St. Petersburg: V. V. Komarov, 1901.

————. *Маги* [The Magicians] (1901–1916). Also *Les mages* [French]. Pentalogy.

Vol. 1: *Жизненный эликсир* [The Elixir of Life] (1901). St. Petersburg: Типография В. В. Комарова, 1901. *Эликсиръ жизни*. St. Petersburg: L. V. Gutman, 1910. Berlin: O. D'iakova, [n.d.] *L'Élixir de longue vie: les immortels sur la terre* [French]. Transl. by Marc Semenof. Paris: Gallimard, 1928. *Еликсирът на безсмъртието / Във вихъра на страстта* [Bulgarian] [n.p.]: M.-L., 1992. *The Elixir of Long Life* [English]. Adapted by Beatriz Stella Limeira. [n.p.]: World Spiritist Institute, 2023.

Vol. 2: *Маги : роман* [The Magicians: A Novel] (1902). Berlin: O. D'iakov, [1923]. Berlin: O. D'iakov, [192-?]. Vachendorf: Strelbytskyy Multimedia

Publishing, 2017 [e-book]. *Magicians: Dedication* [English]. [n.p.]: [n.d.] [e-book].

Vol. 3: ———. *Гнѣв Божій : оккультный романъ* [The Wrath of God: An Occult Novel] (1910). St. Petersburg: Sviet, [1909–]1910. *Гнев Божий* [Russian]. [n.p.]: [n.p.], 2001.

Vol. 4: *Смерть планеты* [Death of a Planet]. St. Petersburg: L. V. Gutman, 1911. Riga: N. Gudkov, 1929. Riga: Vieda, 1992. Vachendorf: Strelbytskyy Multimedia Publishing, 2017 [e-book]. Moscow: Amrita, 2019.

Vol. 5: *Законодатели* [The Lawgivers] (1916). St. Petersburg: [n.p.], 1916. Riga: N. Gudkov, 1930.

———. *На сосѣдней планетѣ : роман* [On the Neighboring Planet: A Novel] (1903). Editions include: St. Petersburg: Knigoizdatel'skoe tovarishchestvo, 1912. Riga: N. Gudkov, [1928].

———. *С неба на землю : миѳ* [From Heaven to Earth: A Myth]. St. Petersburg: V. V. Komarov, 1903.

———. *Свѣточи Чекіи: историческій роман из эпохи пробуждения чешскаго національнаго самосознанія* [The Torchbearers of Bohemia: A Historical Novel from the Era of the Czech National Awakening] (1904). St. Petersburg: V. V. Komarov, 1904. *Светочи Чехии* [Russian]. [n.p.]: Sed'maia kniga, 2014. *The Torch-Bearers of Bohemia* [English]. London: Chatto & Windus, 1916. New York: R. M. McBride, 1917.

———. *Служители зла Люциферьияне* [Luciferians: Servants of Evil]. [n.p.]: [n.p.], 1904.

———. *Мертвая петля* [The Loop] (1906). Editions include: Riga: Skif, 1931.

———. *На Москве : Сон в осеннюю ночь* [In Moscow: An Autumn Night's Dream] (1906). Moscow: Universitetskaia tip., 1906. Vachendorf: Strelbytskyy

Multimedia Publishing, 2017 [e-book].

———. *Новый вѣк : историческая повѣсть* [The New Age: A Historical Tale]. St. Petersburg: [n.p.], 1906.

———. *Паутина : роман в четырех частях* [The Web: A Novel in Four Parts]. [n.p.]: [n.p.], 1906. St. Petersburg: Sviet, 1908. San Francisco: Globus, [n.d.] (reprint).

———. *Болотный цвѣтокъ* [Marsh Flower] (1907). Moscow: [n.p.], 1907. Riga: N. Gudkov, 1929.

———. *Фараон Мернефта* [Pharaoh Mernefta] (1907). *Фараон Мернефта : историческій роман* [Russian]. St. Petersburg: Sviet, 1907. *Le pharaon Mernephtah roman de l'ancienne Égypte*. Paris: A. Ghio, [n.d.]

———. *Бенедиктинское аббатство* [The Benedictine Abbey] (1908). *L'abbaye des Bénédictins*. Paris: E. Dentu, [n.d.] *Бенедиктинское аббатство* [Russian]. Moscow: Terra, 1996.

———. *Въ иномъ мірѣ* [Otherwise]. St. Petersburg: L. V. Gutman, 1910. Riga, N. Gudkov, 1929.

———. *Дочь колдуна : оккультный романъ* [The Sorcerer's Daughter] (1913). Berlin: O. D'iakov, 1927. *The Sorcerer's Daughter* [English]. [n.p.]: World Spiritist Institute, 2023.

———. *Ксенія (Голгофа женщины) : романъ* [Kseniia (A Woman's Golgotha): A Novel] (1917). Riga: D. Tsymlov, 1927. Kharkov: Tavrida, 1993.

———. *Рай без Адама : роман* [Paradise Without Adam: A Novel]. St. Petersburg: Knigoizdatel'skoe tvorchestvo, 1917. Riga: Obshchedostupnaia biblioteka, [193-?].

———. *Во власти прошлаго : романъ* [In the Power of the Past: A Novel]. Berlin: O. D'iakov, [1923].

———. *Немезида : роман* [Nemesis: A Novel]. Riga: Izd. M. Didkovskago, 1925.

———. *В царстве тьмы* [In the Realm of Darkness]. Trilogy.

Vol. 1: *Грозный призрак* [The Terrible Ghost] (1927). Moscow: [n.p.], 1927. Riga: Izd. M. Didkovskago, [193?]. Riga: M. Didkovskii, [1930].

Vol. 2: В *Шотландском замке : Оккультный роман* [In a Scottish Castle: An Occult Novel] (1929). Moscow: [n.p.], 1929. Riga: Izd. M. Didkovskago, 1929.

Vol. 3: *Из царства тьмы : оккультный роман* [From the Realm of Darkness: An Occult Novel] (1929). Riga: Izd. M. Didkovskago, 1929. *В царстве тьмы* [Russian]. [n.p.]: [n.p.], 1999.

———. *Заговоръ: роман* [Conspiracy: A Novel]. Riga: Obshchedostupnaia biblioteka, [1930].

———. *Месть : роман* [Revenge: A Novel]. Riga: Izd. M. Didkovskago, 1930.

———. *Адон : роман* [Adon: A Novel]. Riga: Izd. M. Didkovskago, 1931.

———. *Вампиръ : романъ* [Vampire: A Novel]. Riga: Obshchestdostupnaia biblioteka, [1931].

———. *Кобра Капелла : роман* [Cobra Capella: A Novel]. Riga: Izd. M. Didkovskago, 1931. Riga: Renaissance, [193-?].

———. *Рафаэла: роман* [Rafaela: A Novel]. Riga: Izd. M. Didkovskago, 1931.

———. *Злой дух : повесть* [Evil Spirit: A Story]. Riga: Mir, 1932.

———. *Пауки : роман* [Spiders: A Novel]. Riga: Parsla, 1932.

———. *Блаженны нищіе духом : роман* [Blessed Are the Poor in Spirit: A Novel]. Riga: N. Gudkov, [193-?].

———. *Жгучая страсть: роман* [Burning Passion: A Novel]. Riga: Obshchedostupnaia biblioteka, [193-?].

———. *Чародѣй Мемфиса : роман* [The Sorcerer of Memphis]. Riga: Akademiia, [193-?].

———. *Тайная помолвка* [The Secret Engagement]. Kharkiv: Klub semeinogo dosuga, 2015.

———. *Mihklainee noseegumi. (Welna ligsda): romans* [Mysterious Crimes (The Devil's Nest): A Novel] [Latvian]. Riga: A. Lanzis, [192-?].

———. *Mihla wisu peedewa; romans* [Love Forgave All: A Novel] [Latvian]. [Riga]: A. Lahnis [*sic*], [1930].

———. *Sirds warâ; romans* [The Heart's Power: A Novel] [Latvian]. Riga: A. Lahzis [*sic*], [1930].

———. *Grehks; romans* [A Sin: A Novel] [Latvian]. Riga: J. Burgers, 1932.

———. *Baigais mīlētājs; romans* [The Frightening Lover: A Novel] [Latvian]. Riga: Latgrāmata, [1933].

———. *Svelmainā kaisle: romans* [Ardent Passion: A Novel] [Latvian]. Riga: Latgrāmata, 1933.

———. *L'Enfant de l'abîme* (Ребенок бездны, Child of the Abyss) [n.d.]

———. *L'Ange de l'étoile du matin* (Ангел утренней звезды, Child of the Morning Star) [n.d.]

———. *Les deux soeurs* (Две сестры, Two Sisters) [n.d.]

Elisabeth of Wied, Pauline Elisabeth Ottilie Luise zu Wied (pseud. Carmen Sylva) (1843–1916) [Romania]. First queen of Romania, prolific author of works including fairy tales. Born into German nobility (House of Hohenzollern-Sigmaringen).

Elisabeth of Wied, Pauline Elisabeth Ottilie Luise zu Wied. *Pelesch im Dienst: Ein sehr langes Märchen für den Prinzen Heinrich XXXII. von Reuss* [Pelesch on Duty: A Very Long Fairy Tale for Prince Heinrich XXXII von Reuss]. Bonn: Verlag von Emil Strauss, 1888.

———. *Legends from River and Mountain.* Co-authored with lady-in-waiting Alma Strettell. New York: Dodd, Mead, 1896; and London: G. Allen, 1896.

—————. *The Child of the Sun: Royal Fairy Tales and Essays by the Queens of Romania, Elisabeth (Carmen Sylva, 1843–1916) and Marie (1875-1938)*. Edited by Silvia Irina Zimmermann. Berlin: Ibidem Verlag, 2020.

For other titles by Elisabeth of Wied, see Online Books: https://onlinebooks.library.upenn.edu/webbin/book/lookupname?key=Carmen%20Sylva%2C%201843-1916

Additional resource: *The Child of the Sun* [Kindle edition]: https://www.amazon.com/Child-Sun-Elisabeth-1843-1916-1875-1938-ebook/dp/B08BK3J5FH/.

Blavatsky, Helena (1831–1891) [Russian-American]. Spiritualist, co-founder and leading theoretician of Theosophical Society in New York City in 1875.

> Blavatsky, H. P. *Nightmare Tales*. London: Theosophical Publishing Society, 1892. Note antecedent for "The Ensouled Violin" (pgs. 98–132) in E. T. A. Hoffmann's "Rat Krespel" (1819), translated into English as "The Cremona Violin" (1908): https://www.gutenberg.org/ebooks/44559.

Zaleska de domo Perłowska, Maria Julia (1831–1889) [Poland (Russian Empire)]. Fantastic literature writer.

> Zaleska de domo Perłowska, Maria Julia. *Niezgodni królewicze i królowa perłowego pałacu: bajki prawdą przeplatane* [Dissident Princes and the Queen of the Pearl Palace: Fairy Tales Intertwined with Truth]. Kraków: Nakład Gebethnera i Wolff, 1899. http://polona.pl/preview/35d01311-5901-4ff0-b951-8f75a06ce2c7

Gippius, Zinaida (1864–1945) [Russian]. Wrote in a metaphysical vein, "Russia's first feminist," an author of poetry, plays, novels, short stories, and essays. Concerned with ethical and spiritual renewal, the "new person." More sympathetic to the symbolists than the Decadents. See also: https://www.encyclopedia.com/women/encyclopedias-almanacs-transcripts-and-maps/gippius-zinaida-1869-1945.

Gippius, Zinaida Nikolaevna. *Third Book of Stories*. [n.p.], 1902. Explores mystical and metaphysical themes.

———. *Алый меч* [The Scarlet Sword]. St. Petersburg: M. V. Pirozhkov, 1906. Short stories exploring the author's metaphysics in light of neo-Christian themes.

———. "Он—белый" [He is White]. In *Лунные муравьи* [Moon Ants] (1910). Editions include: Moscow: Al'tsiona, 1912. Russian text: http://az.lib. ru/g/gippius_z_n/text_0370.shtml.

———. "Живые и мертвые" [The Living and the Dead] (1897). Russian text: http://az.lib.ru/g/gippius_z_n/ text_0300.shtml. In *Selected Works of Zinaida Gippius*. Edited by Temira Pachmass. Champaign [Illinois]: University of Illinois Press, 1973. Published the same year as Stoker's *Dracula*. The devil often figures in her work in an ambiguous and not always negative way. Her goal, however, is to comment on the decadence of the period with the goal of renewing or reimagining a "new" kind of religious experience that is neo-Platonic or gnostic.

———. *Зелёное кольцо* [The Green Ring]. St. Petersburg: Ogni, 1916. Play dedicated to "the people of tomorrow." Russian text: http://az.lib.ru/g/gippius_z_n/text_0230. shtml. In English as *The Green Ring: A Play in Four Acts. Authorised Translation from the Russian of Zinaida Hippius. Translated by S. S. Koteliansky.* (London: C. W. Daniel, Ltd., 1920): https://archive.org/details/ greenringplayinf00gippuoft/page/n9/mode/2up.

For a Gippius bibliography (in Russian), see http://az.lib.ru/g/ gippius_z_n/.

Podlipská, Sofie (1833–1897) [(Czech lands) Austria-Hungary]. Stories of romantic love and historical fiction set in the Czech lands; sister of Czech writer Karolina Světlá.

Podlipská, Sofie. "Náměsíčná" [The Sleepwalker]. In *Láska budoucnosti a jiné práce* [A Love of the Future and

Other Works]. Prague: Česká grafická unie, 1903. Romantic tale of a Moon-dweller and an Earth woman.

————. "Vyhlídka do pekla." In *Paměť a smrt a jiné novely* [Memory and Death and Other Stories]. Prague: Česká grafická unie, 1903. A doctor's elderly patient experiences vision of a strange otherworld. In English as "A View into Hell." Translated by Carleton Bulkin. *Journal Hélice: Critical thinking on speculative fiction* 8, no. 2 (winter-spring 2022/3): 157–66. https://www.revistahelice.com/revista_textos/n_33/Helice33-Recuperados-Podliska-ViewHell.pdf.

von Suttner, Bertha (Baroness) (1843–1914) [Austria-Hungary]. First woman to win the Nobel Peace Prize (1905).

von Suttner, Bertha. *Der Menschheit Hochgedanken, Roman aus der nächsten Zukunft* [The High Thoughts of Mankind, Novel from the Near Future]. Berlin-Wien-Leipzig: Verlag der "Friedens-Warte," [1911]. Translated into English by Nathan Haskell Dole as *When Thoughts Will Soar: A Romance of the Immediate Future*. Boston: Houghton Mifflin, 1914. https://archive.org/details/whenthoughtswill00suttiala/

Vrbová, Amálie (pseud. Jiří Sumín) (1863–1936) [Czech lands (Austria-Hungary)]. Moravian author of realistic prose, often with a feminist slant.

Vrbová, Amálie. *Kroky osudu* [The Tread of Fate]. Prague: Vilímek, 1912. Short stories, including "Až za hrob" [Beyond the Grave], a ghost tale.

————. *Povídky skoro o neuvěřitelné* [Almost Unbelievable Stories]. Olomouc: Promberger, 1918. Short stories.

————. *Bílý ďábel* [The White Devil]. [n.p.], 1922. Short stories.

Marie of Romania, Princess Marie Alexandra Victoria of Edinburgh (1875–1938) [Romania]. Last queen of Romania, author of fairy tales. Born into the British royal family.

Marie of Romania. *The Lily of Life: A Fairy Tale by the Crown Princess of Roumania, with a Preface by Carmen Sylva*. London: Hodder and Stoughton, 1913.

―――. *The Child of the Sun: Royal Fairy Tales and Essays by the Queens of Romania, Elisabeth (Carmen Sylva, 1843-1916) and Marie (1875-1938)*. Edited by Silvia Irina Zimmermann. Berlin: Ibidem Verlag, 2020. https://www.amazon.com/Child-Sun-Elisabeth-1843-1916-1875-1938-ebook/dp/B08BK3J5FH/

For other titles, see also Online Books: https://onlinebooks.library.upenn.edu/webbin/book/lookupname?key=Marie%2C%20Queen%2C%20consort%20of%20Ferdinand%20I%2C%20King%20of%20Romania%2C%201875-1938

Procházková, Emilie (née Nováková) (1878–1960) [Czech lands (Austria-Hungary)]

Procházková, Emilie. "Mysterie života: pouť ducha říší astrální" [The Mystery of Life: A Spirit's Journey through the Astral Realm]. *Edice spirit*, vol. 2. Nová Paka: Karel Sezemský, 1917. http://spiritismus.wz.cz/soubory/K.%20Sezemsky%20E.%20Prochazkova%20-%20Mysterie%20zivota.pdf.

―――. *V koloběhu světů* [As Worlds Circulate] (1920–2). Hexalogy.

Vol. 1: *Komtesa Ester* [Countess Esther]. Prague: Česká společnost theosofická, 1920.

Vol. 2: *Róza, pokračování Komtesy Ester* [Rosa, A Sequel to Countess Esther]. Prague: Česká společnost theosofická, 1920.

Vol. 3: *Uran, část první* [Uranus, Part One]. Prague: Česká společnost theosofická, 1922.

Vol. 4: *Uran, část druhá* [Uranus, Part Two]. Prague: Zmatlík a Palička, 1922.

Vols. 5–6: *V moři plamenů* [In the Sea of Flames] and *Země ohně* (Saturn) [Land of Fire (Saturn)]. Prague: Zmatlík a Palička, 1922.

———. *Marťané* [The Martians]. Prague: Zmatlík a Palička, 1922. In English as *The Martians*. Translated by Carleton Bulkin. Joshua Tree [California]: Space Cowboy Books, 2024.

———. *Pan Řehoř* [undated manuscript]. Apparently lost; referred to in a postcard by the author to another writer, archived in the Czech Památník národní písemnictví (Museum of Czech Literature).

Jurić, Marija (pseud. Zagorka) (1873–1957) [Croatia (Yugoslavia)]. First Croatian woman journalist; activist for women's rights.

Jurić, Marija. *Crveni ocean* [The Red Ocean]. Originally published serially in the journal *Jutarnji list,* 1918-1919. Published in two parts: Zagreb: Jutarnjilist, [2015]. Adventure novel with fantastic elements.

Jesenská, Růžena (1863–1940) [Czech lands (Czechoslovakia)]. Influenced by the Decadents.

Jesenská, Růžena. "Duše" [The Spirit]. In *Pohledy do duší: povídky a novely* [Views of the Soul: Stories and Novellas]. Prague: Otto, 1920. A Prague violinmaker makes an instrument containing the soul of his daughter, who can dance beautifully only when it is played but is otherwise lifeless. Note antecedent in E. T. A. Hoffmann's "Rat Krespel" (1819), translated into English as "The Cremona Violin" (1908).

———. [The Mysterious Encounter]. In *Pohledy do duší: povídky a novely* [Views of the Soul: Stories and Novellas]. Prague: Otto, 1920. Adapted from "The Ninth Wave" (1907) by William Sharp (pseud. Fiona Macleod) (1855–1905).

Nyklesová-Bukovanská, Josefina (1888–1954) [Czech lands (Czechoslovakia)]

Nyklesová-Bukovanská, Josefina. *Devět a každá jiná* [Nine and Each One Different]. Prague: [self-published], 1931. Short stories previously published in newspapers including *Lidové listy* and *Smích republiky*; e.g., the comic fantasy "Marconiho telefon s Marsem" [Marconi's Telephone with Mars] from *Smích republiky* 2, no. 6 (6 February 1920); and the story "Vzácná návštěva" [A Distinguished Visitor] from *Lidové listy* (1925) (comic fantasy).

Tilschová, Anna Maria (1873–1957) [Czech lands (Austria-Hungary)]

Tilschová, Anna Maria. "Podivuhodná příhoda" [A Remarkable Incident]. In *Černá dáma a tři povídky* [The Black Lady and Three Stories]. Prague: Šolc a Šimáček, 1924. After an affair with her husband's brother, who then dies, a woman finds her husband transmogrifying into that brother. Translated by Geoff Chew in the collection *And My Head Exploded* (London: Jantar, 2018). Realism with fantastic element.

Kempner, Magda (1894–fall 1944) [Hungary (Transylvania, part of Romania after 1918)]. Educator, poet, writer. Died at Auschwitz.

Kempner, Magda. *Integrállények* [Integral Creatures]. In series Korunk konyvtára [Library of Our Time], no. 4. Cluj-Kolozsvár: Korunk, 1926. https://adtplus.arcanum. hu/hu/view/Korunk_1926/?pg=266&layout=s

von Harbou, Thea (1888–1954) [Germany]

von Harbou, Thea. *Metropolis: Roman* [Metropolis: A Novel]. Berlin: A. Scherl, 1926. Published in serial form in the magazine *Illustriertes Blatt* in 1925. Various English translations; note *Metropolis: New Revised Edition*. [U.S.]: CreateSpace Independent Publishing Platform, 2013.

————. *Die Frau im Mond: Roman* [The Woman in the Moon: A Novel]. Berlin: A. Scherl, [1928]. Translated into English by the Baroness Bettina von Hutten as *The Girl in the Moon*, New York: World Wide Publishing Co., [1930]; and by Ivor and

Deborah Rogers as *The Rocket to the Moon*, Boston: Gregg Press, 1977.

Vavřínová, Anna [dates unknown] [Czech lands (Czechoslovakia)]. Possibly a pseudonym of Emilie Procházková.

Vavřínová, Anna. *Jeanne d'Arc: Panna Orleánská* [Jeanne d'Arc: The Maid of Orléans]. [Nová Paka]: Karel Sezemský, 1926.

Buyno-Arctowa, Maria Jadwiga (1877–1952) [Poland]

Buyno-Arctowa, Maria Jadwiga. *Wyspa mędrców* [Island of Sages]. 4 vols. [n.p.]: [n.p.], 1929–1930. Republished, Warsaw: Alfa, 1991.

———. *Zielony szaleniec* [Green Madman]. Warsaw: M. Arcta, 1933.

———. *Dziecko morza* [Child of the Sea]. Warsaw: [M. Arcta], 1934.

Pražáková, Klára (1891–1933) [Czech lands (Czechoslovakia)].

Pražáková, Klára. *Objev: Komedie o třech dějstvích s předehrou* [The Discovery: A Comedy in Three Acts with a Prologue]. Bratislava: Krásná kniha, 1930. Play about a future technological discovery.

Vlaškovská-Mořkovská, Marie (pseud. Marie Příleská) (1882–1963) [Czech lands (Czechoslovakia)].

Vlaškovská-Mořkovská, Marie. *Očkování proti lásce: Veselohra o třech dějstvích* [Inoculation Against Love: A Comedy in Three Acts]. Prague: Evžen J. Rosendorf, [1931]. Play with a biological-fantastic subject.

Kosáryné Réz, Lola (1892–1984) [Hungary]. Full name Jánosné Kosáry Réz, Eleonóra Mária Anna. Popular author of novels for young readers; translator of Agatha Christie, Pearl Buck, and Margaret Mitchell's *Gone with the Wind*.

Kosáryné Réz, Lola. *Kampa Daria naplója* [The Diary of Daria Kampa]. 1932–49. Unpublished and frequently rewritten. "A sensitive teacher living on the planet

Taluna, threatened by overpopulation. A nuclear-powered spacecraft is sent to Taluna in another solar system, populated by societies of both human beings and super-ants. This land of love and goodness becomes a slave society and a dictatorship of red and black ants." https://www.freeweb.hu/iratok/irodalom/scifi/scifihungarian.htm

Poppeová, Marie (1856–1938) [Czech lands (Czechoslovakia)].

Poppeová, Marie. *Šťastní Zálesníčkové* [The Happy Zálesníčeks]. [Prague]: J. Kober, 1933. Utopia/lost-world novel.

Valentová, Míla (birth/death unknown) [Czech lands (Czechoslovakia)].

Valentová, Míla. *Jehova a mamon* [Jehovah and Mammon]. Mukačevo: Novina, 1934/5. Social novel set in the Jewish community of Subcarpathian Ruthenia, part of Czechoslovakia between the wars.

Urbanová, Růžena (Rossita) Charlotta (née Milfaitová) (1888–1978) [Czech lands (Czechoslovakia)]. Painter, journalist, photographer, world traveler, collector, author.

Urbanová, Růžena (Rossita) Charlotta. *Le Mystère de la cité sous-marine, roman d'aventures* [The Mystery of the Underwater City: An Adventure Novel]. Cover illustration by Cyril Bouda. Paris: Milfait, 1935; and Prague: G. Voleský/Československá grafická unie, 1935. Vernesque novel, published in French in Prague and Paris. In BnF catalog under author name "Urbanová, R. Ch.": https://catalogue.bnf.fr/ark:/12148/cb31519565p

————. *L'Oiseau blanc* [The White Bird]. Apparently written in French in 1937. Published serially in Prague in Czech as *Bílý pták* in *Vlasta* (1947), nos. 2–16. Fantastic novel set in the future; author expresses her fears about Czechoslovakia's fate; novel's title is also the name of the biplane that disappeared over the Atlantic in an attempted Paris-New York flight in 1927. https://books.google.cz/books?id=XFbzDwAAQBAJ&pg=PA548

Brill-Novotná, Růžena (1908–1944) [Czech lands (Czechoslovakia)]

Brill-Novotná, Růžena. *Rekord Henryho Laurenta: letecký román* [Henry Laurent's Record: A Novel of Aviation]. Prague: Rebec, 1936.

Karlin, Alma Ida Willibalde Maximiliana (1889–1950) [Slovenia (Yugoslavia)]. Traveler, author, poet, collector, polyglot, theosophist; one of first European women to circle the globe.

Karlin, Alma Ida Willibalde Maximiliana. *Isolanthis: Roman vom Sinken eines Erdteils* [Isolanthis: A Novel of the Sinking of a Continent]. Leipzig: Grethlein, 1936. In Slovenian as *Isolanthis: roman o potopu celine.* Ljubljana: Sanje, 2012. Reissued in German by Lindenbaum Verlag GmbH in 2021 with secondary title *Roman vom Untergang Atlantis* [A Novel of the Fall of Atlantis], edited by Karl Maria Guth. Atlantis novel with theosophical elements.

Scheinpflugová, Olga (1902–1988) [Czech lands (Czechoslovakia)]. Married to Czech author Karel Čapek.

Scheinpflugová, Olga. *Chladné světlo: Mužská komedie o třech dějstvích* [A Cold Light: A Masculine Comedy in Three Acts]. Prague: A. Neubert, 1936. Play about a future technological discovery.

———. *Acheirové* [The Acheirs]. Serialized in *Svět práce* [The World of Labor] (1948), nos. 1–11. A wartime generation's sins are visited on its children. Dystopian novella.

Grubhofferová, Marie (1901–1977) [Czech lands (Czechoslovakia)]

Grubhofferová, Marie. *Prázdniny ve hvězdách* [Holiday among the Stars]. Prague: Alois Hynek, 1937.

———. *Mezihvězdní piráti* [Interstellar Pirates]. Prague: Sběratel, 1939.

Běhounková, Ludmila (pseud. V. S. Martin) (1908–1976) [Czech lands (Czechoslovakia)]

Běhounková, Ludmila. *Boj o zeměkouli* [The Fight for the Globe]. *Rodokaps*, no. 237. Prague: Rodokaps, 1939. Won second prize in a Rodokaps contest.

Caba, Olga (1913–1995) [Romania]. Born in Subcarpathian Ruthenia, today in Ukraine. Author, poet, teacher.

Caba, Olga. "Ondinele" [Undine]. In *Gândirea* 20, no. 8 (October 1941): 412–6. https://documente.bcucluj.ro/web/bibdigit/periodice/gandirea/1941/BCUCLUJ_FP_279471_1941_020_008.pdf An unidentified narrator travels under the seven seas with an undine.

———. "Scoici" [Shells]. In *Gândirea* 21, no. 5 (May 1942): 241–7. A conversation between a modern female tourist in Capri and a siren, who tells her that the god Pan died only when he saw the first steamship.

———. *Totaliter aliter* [Totally Different]. Bucharest: Cartea Românească, 1982.

———. *Nuvele fantastice* [Fantastic Short Stories]. Bucharest: Cartea Românească, 1984. Includes a revised version of "Shells."

Sečová, Jana (birth/death dates unknown) [Czech lands (Czechoslovakia)].

Sečová, Jana. *Osamělý dům* [The Lonely House]. *Moderní romány*, vol. 142. Prague: F. Svoboda, [1941]. Novella with fantastic element(s).

Tippmannová, Marie (1908–1976) [Czech lands (Czechoslovakia)]. Author of children's literature.

Tippmannová, Marie. *Honzovo perpetuum mobile* [Honza's Perpetual-Motion Machine]. Prague: B. Smolíková-Mečířová, 1944. Moralistic tale of a poor rural youth who through diligent study and experimentation succeeds in patenting a fantastic perpetual-motion threshing machine—and even marries the factory owner's daughter.

Szepes, Mária (1908–2007) [Hungary]

Szepes, Mária. *A vörös oroszlány* [The Red Lion]. Budapest: [unknown], 1946. All known original copies destroyed. Republished in Hungarian as *A vörös oroszlány: fantasztikus regény*, Budapest: Kozmosz, 1984. Translated into German as *Der rote Löwe*, München: Heyne, 1993 [print], München-Zürich: Piper, 2004 [print] and 2017 [e-book]; into English as *The Red Lion: The Elixir of Eternal Life, An Alchemist Novel*, Yelm [Washington]: Horus, 1997; and into Romanian as *Leul rosu*, Brasov: Mix, 2002. A tale of alchemy, transmutation, and spiritual awakening through the esoteric arts.

————. *Sonnenwind* [Solar Wind]. [n.p.]: [n.p.], [ca.1980s].

————. *Der Zauberspiegel* [The Magic Mirror]. [n.p.]: [n.p.], [ca.1980s].

————. *Märchenland Gondwana* [Fairyland Gondwana]. [n.p.]: [n.p.], [ca.1980s].

My sincere thanks to Ivan Adamovič, Maria Carlson, Melvyn Clarke, Máté Hegedűs, Přemysl Houžvička, Mariano Martín Rodríguez, Tony Mileman, Jaroslav Olša, Jr., and Bence Pinter for several suggestions toward this partial list.

Carleton Bulkin

Partial List of Sources:

Adamovič, Ivan. "Bibliografie české science fiction od počátků do roku 2013." In *Na konci apokalypsy: Kronika české science fiction 3: Od Ondřeje Neffa do současnosti*: 523–53. Prague: Plus, 2014.

Antoš, Matěj. "Aspekt genderové identity v žánru gotického románu a identita hrdinek ve vybraných prózách Miloše Urbana." https://www.ceeol.com/search/viewpdf?id=533809.

Badea-Gheracostea, Cătălin. "Short (Hi)Story of Romanian Speculative Fiction: Told for Strangers, Aliens and Secluded Scholars" 2012. https://internationalsf.files.wordpress.com/2012/05/cc483tc483lin-badea-short-history-of-romanian-speculative-fiction.pdf.

Škerij, Nena. "Science Fiction, Fantasy and Horror Literature in Slovenia." March 25, 2019. Translated by Urša Vidic. http://press.futurefire.net/2019/03/speculative-fiction-in-slovenia.html.

Žiljak, Aleksandar. "Science Fiction in Croatia." https://internationalsf.wordpress.com/2012/05/14/new-isf-article-science-fiction-in-croatia-by-aleksandar-ziljak/.

Also of Interest:

Lemann, Natalia. "Wielka cisza w (polskim) kosmosie—(nie)obecność kobiet w polskiej fantastyce socjologicznej doby PRL." [The Great Silence in (Polish) Outer Space—Social Science Fiction in the Polish People's Republic With(out) Women.] *Kultura popularna* 40 (2014), no. 2. https://www.ceeol.com/search/article-detail?id=159410.

Menzel, Birgit. "Russian Science Fiction and Fantasy Literature." https://www.academia.edu/15357182/Russian_Science_Fiction_and_Fantasy_Literature. Mentions Russian women writers Olga Larionova (b. 1935), [Natalya?] Goncharova [1881–1962], Ariadna Gromova (1916–1981), and Valentina Zhuravleva (1933–2004). All published their first works after 1950.

About the Translator

Carleton Bulkin is an independent scholar and translator who holds a master's degree in Slavic languages and literatures from Indiana University. He has lived in Prague, Havana, Moscow, Budapest, Kabul, Rabat, Jeddah, and the Washington D.C. area. Among his publications is the first bidirectional Dari-English/English-Dari dictionary. He currently resides in Seattle.

SPACE
COWBOY

9 798989 630837